THE DEATH OF
SWEET MISTER

A Novel

DANIEL WOODRELL

Praise For Daniel Woodrell

"A dark, disturbing beauty of a story . . . Woodrell throws down sentences that will leave you amazed."

— Charles Frazier

"I can't remember coming across a more precise evocation of innocence lost since Golding's *The Lord of the Flies*. With *The Death of Sweet Mister*, Daniel Woodrell has written his masterpiece - spare, dark, and incandescently beautiful. It broke my heart."

— Dennis Lehane

"Daniel Woodrell's *The Death of Sweet Mister* is nakedly honest, unsettling, pitch perfect, and uniquely American. Put it on the shelf alongside Faulkner, Jim Thompson, and Cormac McCarthy. With this one, Mr. Woodrell has earned himself a piece of immortality."

— George P. Pelecanos

"Woodrell is one of the most intense and accomplished practitioners since Jim Thompson. He has achieved a near mastery of style as language, plot, characterization and theme mesh with a seamless power."

— NY Times Book Review

Other Books by Daniel Woodrell

DANIEL WOODRELL

THE DEATH OF SWEET MISTER

A NOVEL

NO EXIT PRESS

Published in 2002 by No Exit Press
18 Coleswood Road, Harpenden, Herts, AL5 1EQ
http://www.noexit.co.uk

© Daniel Woodrell 2001

The right of Daniel Woodrell to be identified as author of this work
has been asserted by him in accordance with the Copyright, Designs &
Patents Act 1988.

A CIP catalogue record for this book is available from the British
Library.

ISBN 1-84243-043-2

2 4 6 8 10 9 7 5 3 1

Typography by Able Solutions (UK) Ltd, Birmingham.
Printed and bound in Great Britain by Biddles Ltd, Guildford.

In memory of Billy M.
and that Second Street kitchen of swag

We know many things about those we love—
things we nevertheless refuse to believe.

—Elias Canetti

Mother is the best bet and
don't let Satan draw you too fast.

—Dutch Schultz
on his deathbed

RED MADE ME GET OUT and paint the truck another color once we'd crossed the state line. His voice to me seemed always to have those worms in it that eat you once you're dead and still. His voice always wanted to introduce me to them waiting worms. He had a variety of ugly tones to speak in and used them all at me on most days. He whipped off a skinny country rock road and dove the truck down a slope of plain young weeds towards a creek that slobbered and swung under some trees for shade and parked. Glenda, which was my mom, rolled between him and me in the cab, smelling of her "tea," as she called her rum and colas, and last night's sweat and this morning's perfume, her head pretty often soft on my shoulder and her breaths going up my nose. The weather had looped around to where it was good again, too good to last long, and had prompted blossoms to unclench and wild flowers to pose tall and prissy amongst the weeds, plus it brought forth song birds and bumble bees and all the likewise shit of spring. The tree patch we'd swung under blocked the eyesight of any decent folks who might pass along on that rock road and gain a curiosity about us if we were available to be seen. Our ways often required us to not be seen. Red had pulled something fairly wrong in a white truck down in Arkansas and wished to be driving a blue one back in Missouri.

"So hop your fat ass out, boy, and start tapin' those newspapers over the windows. I've showed you how before."

"And I learned it when you showed it."

"Well? So set your flab to wigglin' and get out there and go at it, boy."

Glenda listened to him with her eyes shut and her head on my shoulder. Her pale right hand, which was elegant and fast, snapped like a clothespin onto the pudge at my equator and pinched hard, pinched my flab *extra* hard, this pain reminding me silently to stand up tough to her husband.

She said, "Don't belittle him so that way."

He said, "Which way?"

"Shuggie's not fat."

"The hell he ain't."

Glenda sat upright and flubbed her lips, so gorgeous even with a sleepy face and hardly any makeup. She had hair the color they call raven, and it had been back-combed and puffed up and out and sprayed to a certain round firmness. This was her fancy dolled-up style of hair instead of her usual, which was just drooping loose. Glenda never would get too plain or too heavy. Her eyes were of that awful blue blueness that generally attaches to things seen at a distance, far away, far out yonder on the water, or way way up.

"Maybe," she said, "*portly*, but not . . ."

"Aw, *bull*-shit!" Red shoved his door open and it squawked. "Your boy ain't nothin' *but* fat." He slammed the door, then ducked his head in through the window. He looked at her and said, "What in hell are you smilin' about?"

"If only to avoid wrinkle lines," she said, "I have chosen to *appear* happy." She pinched me again and winked my way. Red turned and went to the truck bed and started tossing out tape and paint and papers. "Is there any tea left in my thermos, Shug?"

"Yeah. I mixed it fresh in the parking lot back at that café."

"Hand it here, baby. I hear a thirst stomping towards me, think I best meet it halfway."

I did hand that tea to her, then I did get out and grab up the papers and the tape Red had tossed. I took the papers and spread them over the glass windshield and side windows, then used my teeth to pull the tape loose. The tape rolled out with a sound like sneezes.

Red stood paces from me near the biggest close bush and pissed piss-lashes at it while singing one of those old songs that once in a while showed up on the radio even that year, which was way after them tunes had got stale. The song was of the "Ready Teddy" or "Tutti Frutti" or "Good Golly, Miss Molly" type of olden rhyming rock'n roll. Olden rhyming tunes to which he was yet and forever dedicated, I'd say. I could not say what had got him to singing or why. This trip to Hot Springs was one of those so many many times when him and Glenda were supposed to patch things up between them and get on the level as married folks again, which they never did do.

I'd become thirteen that year and Red was near only the height I was at that age, but a man. He had the muscles of a man and all those prowling hungers and meannesses. You might have taken him to be a wrestler or a Viking or such from the muscles he carried. His hair was the color you'd expect, but a red of so odd a

11

red that it gave a slight comic-book or circus angle to him. You could see skin shine between the hairs of his head, and the thin amount of hairs left were slicked into a bump, a thin bump of hair combed aloft slick like rockin' greasers of the prior decade, to which he was loyal as to style.

He lashed that bush with four or five cups of coffee he'd drunk at breakfast and kept singing. The song was along the lines of "Lawdy Lawdy Clawdy" or some such. He'd sang it before within my hearing but I never paid attention.

Nice and quick I had the driver's window and the windshield covered by newsprint and all taped down by masking tape. This made a darkness in the cab and that got Glenda to slide out, her yellow skirt slipping high on her legs, carrying her silver thermos. She sat on a thick patch of green weeds in the morning sun with her skirt spread ladylike and watched me. She watched me tape the last side window and the rear window, then pick up the paint. It was spray paint, blue, and there was only four dinky cans.

I started spraying at the hood and tried to keep my fingertip light on the trigger but there was a breeze like baby breath and the paint drifted a small amount. At that moment I noted that I'd not taped over the headlights and had speckled them blue some. I rubbed at the speckles with my shirttail and tried to be sneaky about it but Red saw.

"Fat boy! You dumbshit, I'll knock fire from your ass, dig?"

"I'm wipin' it . . . ."

"You stupid twat. You can't do one simple fuckin' thing right, can you?"

"Red? Red, my God, don't talk to our son that way—you'll get him twisted."

"Our son, my ass."

Glenda eased away a little, her eyes on his fists, which could flurry so swift.

Red slapped me on the back of the head.

The idea that Red was my dad was the official idea we all lived behind, but I wouldn't guess that any of us believed it to be an idea you could show proof of or wanted to. I was his only child and likely I wasn't his and that likeliness naturally did not serve to mellow his attitude much. His attitude stayed at simmer or scorch on all subjects that I know of but olden rhyming rock'n roll. He carried young love for that music and some sort of crashed but still moving wrecked love for Glenda, but that was it that I know about.

I taped over the headlights. There wouldn't be enough paint in those cans anyhow. Trucks were of full-grown size back then and four dinky cans wouldn't hardly do a fine job of making a full-grown truck another color from the color it started as.

Glenda raised her face and smelled deep so her chest rose and wiggled nice, and said, "Days such as this don't come in a row much, so you be sure to wallow in this one all you can, sugar."

There *was* a variety of smells that bode well in the air. Cute plants were all about and perky up and down the slopes and gullies. Fine spring days such as that got the animals to frolic and chirp like they'd each just inherited stuff that put them on easy street.

"That's a lot of tea this early," I said. "The rule is lunch first, before tea."

"This is a trip, Shug. There's no rules on trips."

Red spit and scuffed his boots in the dirt.

I sprayed and hunched and watched Glenda lift and pour from the silvery thermos to her silvery cup, then sip. She lived even her goofy moments with style, a strain of bravery showed in the smallest of her acts. She needed to bounce often in her days and knew how to bounce and bounce back, which I never truly did. I dented and rolled but hardly ever bounced in her style, and that did not help.

The color of the truck had halfway become another one, a slight blue with small fades to white. The paint lent a hospital smell to the air. The smell moved along in quick drifts. I got to spraying the fenders, toward the truck bed gate, and this shadow fell beside me so I looked and there stood Red, with his shirt off and his angry face on. His chest hairs were red curls, spongy with sweat even in good weather. His appearance was of someone *so* strong!

"Very sneaky, fatso."

"Huh?"

"When I say fatso, daddy-o, I'm talkin' to you, dig? Ain't you noticed you're fatter'n shit?"

"Uh-huh. But you said sneaky."

He pointed down to the flat of the truck bed. Freckles of paint had blown from where I aimed and come down on the bed. Enough freckles fell that you might say swipes of paint showed.

"You think that'll fool anybody? A shitty job like that? You think a shit job of paintin' like that'll keep me out of the pen if we was to run up on a roadblock, or just get pulled over? I'd have to use this." He bent and thumped his right boot where he kept a secret vicious pistol. "And that'd be uncalled for, and on *your* head, fatso."

Glenda said, "Red, honey, come here."

For her to call him honey hurt both of us but she could see he was clouding up over me. She knew how that went. I knew to be alert for his left fist to come at my tummy. I knew to fall down and act destroyed if the fist landed.

"You'd like it if they run me back to the pen, huh, boy? You'd like to make a couple of fuck-ups that got me a nickel bit in the pen, or more'n that, even. Why not life, huh?"

I never answered, for what deeply stung me that day was when Glenda stood up and swished over and stood between us and did her entire girly-girl act of heaving chest and batted eyes and comely dimples that showed as bookends to her smiles. She leaned against that man and purred. She smelled his chest of wet red hairs and hummed a "My, oh my" hum of girly-girl invitation. She stroked his arm with her lovely fingers.

Finally he took his attention from me and gave it to her. He flicked fingertips at her nipples. She managed a smile and he put a hand under her right tit and bounced it in his palm like a newborn that ain't been burped yet. When she didn't make a face like usual that said go away he reached down and pulled her yellow skirt up and where he touched her and how he touched her made her inviting expression shrink and she said, "Uh, uh—careful. Be careful."

"Or else what?"

I only just stood there, paint can in hand with my mouth probably fallen open.

Then the kissing started, which I know hurt us both.

She wouldn't look at me.

She led him away and in amongst the bushes. I tried to spray. They got back amongst the bushes and I heard the sound of his boots being tugged off. She made grunts when they tugged free. There were a couple of snickers I guess were lusty and a buckle noise. The paint was running out as I sprayed too much at the sky, the grass, my own left hand. I could hear skin slap skin and those various groans. I would have rather took a beating. He thrashed away at her all noisy and in command and she gasped sweet horseshit back to him.

I turned to the truck and pushed the paint trigger.

Screaming just then came loud to my heart but I knew better, I knew better and only hung my head and wished I had fewer ears and kept spraying blue paint.

The screams I bottled that time and all the times similar waited and waited to be loosed, until the time they were.

I wish I could add none of this happened.

L IVING ALONGSIDE THE GATHERED DEAD of our town was a thing me and Glenda never did fear 'cause we never done them no dirt when they lived. That was the notion, anyhow. Glenda said that notion plenty ever since I can recall. At bedtime she said it especially often when I was little. "They're all buried, hon, and they *don't* hate you." Every window we had opened onto a vista of tombstones, which included the window by my bed. I believe dusks and dawns spent staring out that window shaded me ever more towards no-good and lonely. Trees grew in the cemetery too, great hulking oaks and sentinel pines, plus squirrels jigged freely about the grounds, but it's those ranks of tombstones that spook the big lasting impression into a person's mind. When you look there, that's what you see: the dead, long dead and fresh dead and in between.

The dead had been coming to the West Table Cemetery for over a hundred years, since names like Zebediah, Aquilla, and Verity and Permelia had been everyday names in the Ozarks, and Glenda somehow landed a cemetery job that got us a house in the middle of all those dead and their severe olden names. The job was supposed to be her job but soon as I got any size the work got done by us together, her and me. Red used to show up sometimes and help way back, but not after I got size and could mow. A tractor came with the job which Glenda couldn't even get to start.

"Darned ol' thing!" she'd say, so I'd climb on and start it and she'd be amazed yet again and go, "Huh," then watch me drive. The tractor cut the grass around the cemetery and between the tombstone ranks, but the space sideways between tombstones was too tight and I pushed a regular mower there.

Our house looked as if it had been painted with jumbo crayons by a kid with wild hands who enjoyed bright colors but lost interest fast. That kid was me, in general, and I did try any paint we had in the shed. The paint was mostly different stripes of white, plus a bit of yellow, blue, and red. Glenda maybe painted a low corner or a window sash before her tea kicked in and she might drag out a kitchen chair and sit where the shade fell and talk about such subjects as clothes she had once she wished she still did, sweaters, stoles, and silky sorts of stuff, or places she had been escorted to for eats back when and hoped to someday take me to, spiffy tablecloth places in Kentucky and Miami and Cleveland.

Red either was there or he was not and he made it plain it was none of our fucking business which. He kept busy off and away from us with his thieving buddies hunting for soft crimes to pull and maybe some not so soft. When he was home he was never home every day in a row more than three or four days, and when he was not there he might not be for two or three weeks. He'd be gone long enough to get my hopes high, lighten my heart, then I'd hear whichever heap he then drove come grumbling into our drive and dash me again.

THE FIRST PLACE I ROBBED for Red stood tall, set high on a brick wall, and the only way to reach so high on that brick wall was to shinny up the gutterpipe. Red dropped one claw on my shoulder and used the other to point along the brick wall to the window he was sending me to. The shade there hung part down so the window fairly winked a yellowy shade. That window winked at a corner on the third floor of a squatty sour old place with bricks of that worn-out color, a color passing years slap on, three stories in height and set lonesome by the stockyards, sort of asking to be robbed.

"I'm a li'l hefty to climb the whole way up there on that pipe."

"It'll hold."

"Stuff has broke under me before."

"It'll hold," Red said. "If it don't, me and Basil'll be sure and catch you on the way down, hey, Bas'?"

"Oh, yeah. We'll call 'I got it! I got it!' so's we don't collide and make an error."

Red's one claw clenched its nails into my skin.

"That pipe's been holdin' all this century, fat boy, and you ain't so goddamn special it's goin' to fly apart over you. So hush your worryin'."

I looked at that winked window from where I stood, and charted the distance there in my head.

"That could be, uh, forty feet, I think. I think they say that's too many feet to fall, you know, and walk away."

That claw raised from my shoulder and became a fist and bopped down on top of my skull.

"Jesus, you're a pussy," Red said. "That witch has made somethin' purt near *use*-less out of you."

This night was a big-moon night. They shared slugs from a bottle, Red and Basil, gin, I believe. They did shove the clear bottle from one to the other and back for a while, releasing glug-glug sounds and lip squeaks. They had faces washed pale by that big-moon glow. The stockyards lay empty but did remain good and stinky, ankle deep with mush. The two of them and me kind of stood around one of the slat gates to the holding pens, the swinging kind, or else leaned on it. Mosquitoes drilled us in our soft spots and sounds of slapping hands ran across the feedlot one way and towards the town square the other.

Red blew his gin breath low at me, his features taken off by the dark, but I could tell he stared steady. "And if somethin' flew wrong and you got your ass pinched, then what?"

"I'm just a kid," I said in a put-on kid voice. "I'm just a kid out pullin' stupid pranks, Officer. I sure am sorry."

"And if you don't get pinched?"

"Fill this here pillowcase with all the drugs and things I can see."

Basil said, "That means things liquid, too, Shug. Some of the best dopes come in liquid style."

"I been told."

Basil Powney was Red's main cohort in life. They had in common both being a bubble off plumb. They had come along as kids together and gone along to prison almost together, just a month apart 'cause their trials had got split. Basil was a tall narrow fella with ways easy to like. He was tall by nature and kept narrow by dope, I do imagine. His head did not quite fit with his body, being maybe a size small for balancing with that lanky trunk. As to hair and eyes, he was dark. Most often he showed a beard of some kind or went about unshaved, and his teeth shined plenty white as he doted on them. He carried a toothbrush in a hip pocket where most might pack a comb. He scrubbed at his teeth every time you turned around, even when he seemed too drunk to stand or had got hopped up on dope and wanted to get going somewhere. He just about did not ever call me names or get rough in my direction.

"Plus guns," Red said. "If the ol' doc has got any guns they are always welcome."

"I'll look," I said. "If I get there."

"You're gonna *have* to get there."

"Maybe I can."

"*Maybe* gets your butt kicked, dig?"

"I guess."

Car lights ran around and about the night, cars turning corners or rounding bends, letting their beams loose to graze on the dark. Twice I did see smoochy couples paused on the square. A hurt-voiced dog was chained up lonely or locked out not too far away and did bay and bay, baying so's I could understand, baying the way I felt.

Basil said, "Now's good as anytime, Red."

21

"Yup." Red grabbed me and shook me. He handed me a chisel. "Put that in the pillowcase and tie it to your belt."

Before I could get that task done all the way and proper, get the knot snug, he said, "Come on, fat boy, come on—play at bein' a monkey and scoot your ass up that pipe."

The gutterpipe had the color of rust but from paint, paint that had matched the sour old bricks. My hands could just almost join around the pipe. The skin of the pipe was not on there smooth, but had gougy spots of dried gunks, itty-bitty sharp ridges, places that scraped.

"Now what? What's holdin' you now?"

There at the corner of the building the builders had made a sort of design of bricks that left brick lips pouted out every few feet which I could touch my toes on and push, those brick lips and toe pushes being the main reason I did go up the pipe. Pretty quick I had got up to a height I would not want to fall from, unless into water or something softer, and kept on. The pipe let out sounds as I went up, weak, screechy sounds such as olden folk give when the breaths they draw are not full enough and they do try and try for more, those noises of that sort, and now and then something close to a grunt or scold.

"Go, fat boy, go!"

I had come close to the window, close to where I could spit to it, when the pipe buckled. The pipe buckled, grunting and sagging from the wall, but in the main held to the bricks. I did slip and I did clamber and I did say words I do not recall.

"You *ain't* fallin'. You *ain't* fallin'."

I held to the pipe at the sagging spot and held it dear. I could see from there beyond the square to the lights on the hill and the other way to the lights that stood over Broadway and the special light at Dog'N Suds on that street. The wind up there felt glad to meet me.

"You ain't a statue—get goin'."

I had a lost moment in a hope of mine, which was that I would if I could hope to be buried in a tin can. Have the doctor render me to nuggets the size of seeds and put me in an old tin can, the kind with the jagged lid still clinging, and nailed high in a tree so birds will feed on me from the can and then flap and flap and fly all across the globe shitting me on everybody still alive down there. That is the funeral I did hope for at certain times and clung to that gutter I did again. I wanted that tin can nailed about level with where I clung.

"I'm gettin' tired."

"You're what?"

"Tired."

"Naw, not at your age, you ain't. You should never get tired at your age."

"My arms are shiverin'."

"Get on in there—do your job."

Basil said, "You know, Shuggie, remember the Little Train Who Could, right? They still teach that? The little train and the big-ass hill or whatever? Woo! Woo!"

I guess my toes found a brick lip. I guess my arms did shiver and pull, shiver and pull. I know I got to the ledge by the window and reached toes towards it. The ledge was a ledge you could stand on, which I did do. My butt was flush to the glass as I stood to unknot the pillowcase and bring out the chisel.

Along the ground down there Red and Basil goofed about, slap-boxing and like that, and once Red came under a light where I did see him kick the air with his boots that had white wings that started at the point and flared back and feathered, I knew, up to the shin part. The boot wings were intended as white eagle wings. His kicks came and went fast as blinks.

Then him and Basil stood still and whispered a list of what they hoped I might steal for them. The whispers that went back and forth came up so I could hear.

"Redbirds."

"Footballs."

"Dexies."

"Yellowjackets."

"A nice thirty-eight."

"Brompton's punch."

"Tuinals."

The wood of the window had been through a lot, sun and ice, snow and rain, years and years. It did now wiggle in the frame, wiggle loose at the joints, and I poked the chisel at a joint, then went bang with my hand on the chisel, then went bang once more, and those two bangs broke it loose from the frame. The wood came apart easy like pulling baby teeth. One section of glass slid loose, but slid loose all of a piece, and I caught it and carried it inside with me and laid it down whole.

"Hey—I made it! Look at this—I made it!"

"Hush your mouth. When you get back out—*that's* when you made it, dig? *That's* when you crow."

One step inside the window I bumped a desk and then felt of it, scouted my hands about the flat part to hit a lamp, maybe, which happened. I scouted my hands up to the lamp neck but the button wasn't found, so I scouted back to the root and did find the button there and did push it. The light made was plenty.

I took the chisel and used it against everything, popped drawers, popped cabinets, opened desks. Whatever I took to be a pill or bottle of medicine juice or a box that could hold either I dumped into the pillowcase. I dumped until I filled it pretty heavy. When I went to the window and looked down the buckled gutterpipe, the one speaking voice in my mind did say and say, Huh-uh, huh-uh.

IN the car, Red said, "You wasn't supposed to just waltz down the stairs and bust out the fuckin' front door. That wasn't what I fuckin' told you."

Basil did the driving. The car was one I did not know, a white Corvair that sounded like a vacuum cleaner. He was grinning and whistling and tapping his fingers on the wheel. He said, "The boy by God grabbed up all the shit, though. And plenty of that was what we hoped for."

"He was told to come down the goddamn gutter."

Red and Basil had got beer at Slager's. It was the kind of beer they had in those days that came loose in plastic bags, six cans to a bag, and cost the least of any kind. The beer cans popped open and added one more smell to the car that did not set with me. There was the gin, there was the sweat, there was the beer, and there was stinks I could not name. None set with me good.

Finally Red said, "But you did okay. You got plenty."

"Uh-huh. So, what will, uh, will be my share?"

Red twisted to look at me and his face did not look generous.

"Well now, would you just *listen* to fat boy!"

"I just figure I should get a share."

"Not hardly," Red said. "Not in this lifetime."

"Now, I was him," Basil said, "*I'd* figure on a share."

"You ain't even got no kids, so shut the fuck up about it. Dig?"

The Corvair ran us on around town awhile. Streets of quiet, slow cars, houses going dark for sleep. Nobody said anything for some time, a long drinking quiet passed. Those two opened more beers, foamy stink sprayed.

Then Red spoke. "I wanted you to use the gutter, Shug. It was safer. You should know I've got to be mighty careful 'cause of my priors. Those are *always* hangin' over me."

I did not answer except with a nod, which he caught.

Basil said, "Hey, Red—let's us fall on by and visit Patty and them, what say?"

"Pull over, Basil." We were at the graveyard edge, the far edge from the house. Several of my favorite dead ones were laid out right by where the Corvair stopped, dead ones I tended, dead ones I'd sat amongst. Red held the door open so the light on the roof shined, and he yanked open the pillowcase and did run his fingers through the many tinkling handfuls of what I stole. "Not bad. This'll work. You get on out now and walk on home—we need to be somewhere. And if that witch pushes her nose in and asks what we got up to, boy, you just tell her, 'Men stuff.' Not one word more. That's all you need to tell her, 'Men stuff.' She'll hear you."

GLENDA said, "I don't much like the sound of that."

"That's all we did."

"Was he nice to you?"

"Practically."

"Mm-hmm," she went. "I'll bet you could use your snack now, hon, couldn't you?"

"I feel ready for it."

The TV was turned where it always was at this time of a weekday, on that channel she favored, the channel that did go on with the show beyond when people with jobs went to sleep. The show was ol' Johnny and his movie-star friends gassing, mostly. A big fat gray couch tracked back from the TV so a person could lay flat and view the whole screen without spraining their neck. On the floor flopped a beanbag chair, which would act like a horror-movie flower trying to eat you if you sat in it, a bright yellow color. TV trays were stood around and had pictures on the tray parts showing bottles of cola that wore aprons to barbecue or danced in a barn wearing cowboy hats or played badminton at a picnic, the family cola was the kind. Glenda's tea did sit as usual on such a tray, and did lay a puddle there as the ice got smaller.

I sat on the couch turned a nudge towards the screen where a bald cartoon giant spun about in a whir showing an actual human mother how best to clean her house. I could hear my snack being built in the kitchen. There was the icebox sucking shut, the rattle in the knife-fork-spoon drawer looking for the scoop, water coming to a boil.

At night Glenda liked to dress like she had somewhere to go. Somewhere to go where people showed up in high-hat clothes. Glenda wore a cool thin green thing, green as those green jewels, and the thing was bottom and top in one connected piece, and the top left her back skin out altogether and had thin straps that came up in a knot behind her neck. The green thing fit loose low on the legs but fit real huggy at the important other places.

"There, Shug."

The snack came in a batter bowl, and did as always come in the same batter bowl, cherry-colored on the outside and snow white inside around a heap of vanilla ice cream that had got splashed by a cup of coffee to make a sweet mud. When I ate, Glenda, as usual, put an arm around me and held her drink up for sips and acted like we were out for the evening to somewhere else. I kept busy with the spoon, spooning every drop from the batter bowl while her arm lay across my shoulders.

She said, "Now, that man, Shug, I don't think that man is so durn funny. He's just rude, is all. Johnny should boot him."

I leaned to set the empty bowl on a tray and on the tray I spotted a scratch pad all scribbled on in ink that said: "Glinda? Glynda? Glenda Ambers Akins? Gllynda? Glynnda? Glenda Akins?"

A little later Glenda let her head sag to my neck and her breath ran hot along my skin and I swallowed the smell of her and her perfume and tea.

"Man stuff, is it?" she mumbled. "I don't believe that's good news, hon."

4

THE BEST ONES WERE ALWAYS surrounded by stickers. She said that over and again as if those words amounted to an answer. The berries had come up from nubs in the sunshine and rain and come to the good size and ripeness. The sharp stickers on the ropy whips of bushes did their damage, such as short thin scrapes along forearms, points pushed into thumbs, a blow of wind loosing a whip of stickers so it raked a neck or backside. The berries were spotted all about in amongst the thicket of stickers and big numbers of them, too.

The berries were black, the buckets were gray. She had a bucket and I had a bucket and most of the berries in her bucket had got picked by me and each of the ones in my bucket had. My skin showed plenty of tiny blood spots. Small freckles left where small pains had called. The morning weather wasn't so bad. The heat slept in and a wind roamed. The berries could fetch us a price at Lake's Market.

"There just always is stickers around the best ones," Glenda said for the severalth time. "The ones you need to pick."

"Uh-huh."

"You're showin' blood, baby. Blood on your knuckles. On your arms."

"My neck, too. Sweat runs in there and God damn but it stings."

"Don't get yourself overhot, Shug."

We walked together along a lonely road that ran out from that side of town. The road had heavy brownish dust and those chunky rocks on it with edges that can hit tires like tomahawk blades sometimes. Anyplace there were berries we went. I'd straddle the barbed-wire fences and let my fat shove the rusty wires low so she could step over. She'd step over careful 'cause she wore shorts and pick the ones easy to pick along the outside of the thickets. I would get down and crawl into low rough spaces after berries if I saw them and it was like tunnels in there. Tunnels for things way smaller than I and walled in by sharp points that hurt but not enough to make you stop and go away.

There came a time to rest and we sat in the dirt gutter that went alongside the road. We squatted on the high hump with our feet down. I got my knife out and sprang the blade open and sat there slicing the points from a blackberry whip. The buckets stood nearby, gray and getting heavy, almost full.

She said, "Your profile would sure show well on a silver coin, I think."

"I've got a double chin."

"Well. It makes you appear successful, Shug. Worthwhile. Like the prosperous, who eat so good."

"Naw. I'm thirteen, Glenda. It's just fat when you're a teenager."

She made a pout, pooched her lips out plump and pink and turned them down, and her eyes loomed big.

"I guess I have my work cut out, teachin' you to see yourself as I do, hon."

"How's that?"

"As an ace waitin' to be played."

"An ace? Shit—cut the comedy."

She dropped her head so her face and that look of big-eyed pouting could be used on me more.

"You've got so much to live up to, sweet, sweet darlin'. The man whose name you carry stood at the head of the parade. He stood where bosses stand and he stood there big as life, too. He wasn't called the Baron as a joke. Huh-uh, he sure wasn't. He was the man who told you yes or no, sink or swim."

In the woods beyond the spot where we sat little creatures told jokes on the other little creatures and clicked their nails on tree bark and skittered so the leaves waffled and twisted as they laughed their kind of laughs. From somewhere off yonder came a soft mumble of a creek dreaming a good one.

"Did he look like me?"

"No. But you sort of look like him for some reason."

"We're built alike?"

"When you rise two inches taller you'll look so like him my heart'll break again."

This fella the Baron was a fella of legend Glenda came to know, or so I got told, at some stretch of time when Red did not stand at her side twisting her arm. She never said that man was my actual founding daddy, but pounded it at me that I carried his front name, which I did not care for and was Morris.

"What're you doin' with Red, anyhow?"

Glenda got slow to her feet and stretched, her hands palms down at the low spot of her back, shoulders turning this way and that, pushing up and away from the road on tippy-toes so her leg muscles showed sleek. Under her arms her shirt was damp from sweat and probably her shorts should have fallen longer to be classed as motherly.

"Listen," she said. "You might not believe it, but the first time I ever set eyes on Red Akins he looked like a Greek god. *Understand?* A Greek god who was maybe a li'l short, shorter'n you figure most Greek gods stood, and his hair was the color it is and already just a li'l bit thin, but still, you know, he was chiseled together like some daddy god or other had put considerable overtime in on the job of hammerin' *him* out."

I pitched the whip I'd shaved smooth, and closed the knife.

"He still fairly pops with muscles, Mom."

"Oh, I reckon that's so. I reckon it is. But his poppin' muscles don't bring Greek gods to mind anymore."

"How do we stand him?"

"Well," she said. "Well." She picked up a bucket and began a stroll on down the road so I hefted the other and caught up to her. When I did I took her bucket from her and carried both buckets swinging below what I guess were my fat but somewhat strong arms. The buckets felt like spare heads with long hair handles. After we'd kicked a ways down the dusty road she said, "You wake up in this here world, my sweet li'l mister, you got to wake up tough. You go out that front door tough of a mornin' and you stay tough 'til lights out—have you learned that?"

"I think so."

"Hmm. There'll come a time when we'll just see about that. Mm-hmm. I'm dead sure that time is gonna come."

MY mom let men have ideas about her. Some would say me too. She had a way of shuffling generally real loose at the pivot points that made you look when she went by, wherever it was that she went by you: store, alley, roadhouse, country lane. Granny said Mom could make "Hello, there" sound so sinful you'd run off and wash your ears after hearing it, then probably come back to hear it again. I never used the word "sinful" on her in my head. It was just that she was so pretty and willing to smile and fellas got the idea they had a good chance with her when she smiled if they showed a little effort and tickled her some way.

That day of the berries we came to the creek that crosses the rock road at a low-water depth. This was a ways out from town past Venus Holler a distance and from the creek to Lake's Market was likely over a mile.

I set down our buckets and we splashed water at each other. It seemed maybe my flesh had broke quite a few of those sticker teeth from the blackberry lashes as I picked, and Glenda's back seemed like it had also. I pulled my shirt off and she bent to the creek and cupped her hands in the water and raised the cup to my back and let the water run slow across my bloody spots. She repeated that several times and it brought comfort to me.

She said, "You look like cats hate you."

"There's drops of blood on your shirt too, Glenda."

She did then kneel at the creek lip, knees squishing mud, her raven hair a fallen tangle, and did lift the rear of her shirt so I could rinse her back. The sun never worked much tan into her skin, so pale was she forever. The dots of blood had crusted. There was no bra strap where usually there should have been. I did do to her that cup stuff with my hands and the water, poured and poured. The water gushed down from her shoulders and flooded inside her white shorts and waterlogged them.

"That's good," she said. "That's enough. That's fine."

When she stood I could see her panties inside her wet white shorts and I do suppose her panties were entirely wet, too. A flesh tone showed through plus dark patches. She never did lose her figure, which was good to great.

Mom looked at me funny for a spell there, standing in the sunlight so damp and revealed, then laughed.

"What will Lake pay for these berries, Shug?"

"He pays by what they weigh. Let me show you how to do this."

I dropped into a deep squat and scraped together a handful of stones from the creek bed. The stones had a bevy of colors but most all were only shades of white or brown. Some might have been orange-brown, quite a few were cream. It's possible somewhere in the pile were a couple that fit black. Once the handful of stones suited me I duckwalked to the buckets of berries.

"Just pull some up," I said, which I did. I pulled a bunch of berries up in one hand, started dropping stones in with the other. The berries gave out a smell I always felt flush when smelling. "Just put a few stones in the bucket, see. That'll raise your pay when he weighs them. Old man Lake knows how much his buckets weigh, so he just puts it on the scale when you hand it in and does the subtraction and what not to pay you."

"You're a sneaky young shit, ain't you, hon?"

"You raised me," I said. "Don't use big stones—he'll spot those. Just a handful of li'l stones, see, and not on the bottom where they'll clank. Bed them in the middle of the berries and, also, then if he *did* find them, he'd have to wonder if they were there by accident."

"Can you still tote both buckets, hon?"

"Oh, yes ma'am. You bet. I mean, it's not that far, for a *man*, right?"

WE walked home the way we came, which was the long way. The sun had begun to work harder and work us harder, too. Twice we saw snakes drawing spaghetti lines in the dust of the road. One was a bad snake and one was a kind it's supposed to be good to have around. I tried to bean both with rocks but didn't. Glenda had huffed herself several strides ahead of me.

"That was awful," she said. She smoked a cigarette from the pack we bought at Lake's. The brand was one of those he-man brands of smoke, but it had the taste she liked. "That was so low-rent. A grown lady such as me, caught cheatin' on berries!"

"It seems he's learned how I do him."

"Oh, yeah! He's learned, all right."

"I didn't figure he had yet."

"Oh, I ain't going to rag on you for tryin', Shug. Only I shouldn't have stood there, too."

"Uh-huh. Got you those smokes, anyhow."

"Yup. Certainly did do that, okay."

"So why not give *me* a taste of one?"

"Hmm. I don't know about that, Shug. I don't know. Now, the Baron smoked, naturally. Of course, that man had such *fine* taste in so many things, and manners, too. The smooth way he undid a napkin, even, and tucked it in his collar, so high-tone! He'd been places. Places where the good stuff happens. And it is a fact, Shug, the Baron smoked *this* kind."

"That's why I'll try me one, huh?"

She halted and dished a cigarette to me, then held my hand steady so she could put fire to it.

"It's goin'," I said.

Glenda had been sunned dry but dust had settled on her clothes when they were damp and the dust dried a stain on those white shorts so they looked like a dirty coffee cup. She took short steps along the road and hummed to herself. After some steps she'd spring up on one leg and spin on her foot so dust got splashed and rocks rolled away. She had an idea of what moves to make, dance steps she'd once known and done plenty, I reckon.

The smoke she trained me on had a taste that seemed gruff, kind of a big-bully taste, a taste which apparently the Baron favored. She watched me draw in the smoke and pipe it out and when I coughed her eyes narrowed as if she fought against finding me silly, a child, a silly child. I saw myself different by then. I drew in two or three more swallows of smoke real manly and did not cough or turn a bad color and she nodded several satisfied nods my way.

I stamped the butt into the road dust.

"Not bad," I said. "Could be that'll be my kind."

"Oh now, I'd bet on that. I'd bet plenty on that."

Once we reached the creek there was a Thunderbird parked in it. The rear wheels sat dry on the road and the front tires rested in running water up to the hubcaps, which shined. The sunlight hit those hubcaps and bent. The car had the style and reputation that got me and Glenda to pause staring. The color was a special green color called something I don't know. The inside of the car was white in general and factory clean. A barefoot man stood in the water, his pants legs rolled up to the knees. The pants were gray dress pants and he wore a necktie loose around an open white collar. He had crouched over and was sponging and scraping dead bugs from the grille and headlights, flicking them to the creek.

Glenda stalled where she stood. She only moved her eyes while she studied that car, which was of one of the legendary vintages of Thunderbirds. It was the kind you drive in your head. It was the kind most everybody wheeled around in their heads. She just stood there stalled like she was following orders a voice I could not hear had barked to her.

The man in the water looked up and rubbed his hands together with his eyes on Mom. He was a fairly big chubby fella without too much hair growing and what there was seemed basically gray. His hair sat on his head wispy like a dust bunny above the screen door. He stared at her and smiled a smile that twisted way up on one end of his mouth.

I said, "Hey, mister! What the hell you lookin' at?"

"Shoosh, hon—don't address this man that way."

"But I know what he's thinkin'."

"I surely do hope you don't, Shug."

The man said, "How do, folks. No offense meant, kid."

She went into that stall again.

Finally she says, "It's green."

"Uh-huh, it is."

"It's green like the future."

"The future? How is that?"

"The future's still green I imagine, at *this stage*, I mean. Don't you?"

"Oh yeah, uh-huh. Now I get you."

"Come on, Glenda."

Her eyes went on that Thunderbird and lingered.

I pulled her by the hand but she had took root there on that spot. I leaned my head forward and sagged my weight with her hand in mine and got her off balance and she came stumbling along splashing through the creek.

Again she stalled on the other side of the water and turned about to stare.

I put together a long chain of the words "Come on, Glenda, come on, Glenda, come on, Glenda."

I could not say why but suddenly her shoulders fell and she came along meek, me tugging at her hand,

and never said a thing until that rock road had led us home.

5

RED HAD BEAT HIS GUITAR since midnight. Red and Basil had got happy on some kind of dope in the kitchen. They did get happy and the guitar did get beat and parts of songs flew from it. They each smoked cigarettes and burned enough cigarettes to send smoke signals from the kitchen. Their happy had run wild all night and they had not begun yet to fizzle towards bed. By the sun it had turned breakfast time but on their clocks run by dope they seemed to be at another hour, another hour around early night when fun stuff had just got started. The kind of happy they had got was the kind that would get loose and would slop about into the way of everybody else

Red beat old rhyming songs from that box and Basil sort of knew some of the words so he sort of sang them along with Red. Their voices sounded as bloodshot as their eyes. The songs were just parts of songs, the remembered parts of songs that sleep in the head and will come awake when those certain sounds get beat from the box.

A song they went at again and again had a main line about wanting one cup of coffee and a cig-a-rette, and then some other lines Red and Basil made ragged guesses at, ragged different guesses from each made at the same time.

Glenda stood there at the stove not truly dressed for daylight, sweating even so early in the day over the black skillet, melting butter for winkeyes. Sleep had mashed her hairdo lopsided.

"For goodness' sake," she said, "drop that song, would you? Sing something you know the goddamn words to."

The song stopped and I heard the guitar hit the floor and skid.

Red said, "Best keep quiet in the peanut gallery."

To help Glenda cook I stood nearby pinching eyeholes from the center of bread slices. I'd roll the bread from the pinched eyeholes in my fingers, I'd roll it into tight balls like fish bait and go for them each in one gulp.

"I love winkeyes."

"There'll be plenty, hon."

The other two had took more dope, pills which were shook from a rattling bottle, and took to giggling and getting windy with words.

Red said, "I always feel like I own just as far as I can piss in every direction."

"You oughta drink more beer!"

"Yup. I ain't got much, you know, but I'll still fight over it."

"Ain't that the truth! Ain't that the sorry fuckin' truth."

When the butter in the skillet took to hissing and popping inside the bread center Mom would bust an egg and dump it to fill the eyehole, the winkeye hole. The egg roared hitting the hot butter, then cooked fast, and cooked hard and came to look sort of like an eye a dumptruck had run over. I could eat six winkeyes on my sickest day but did not get to usually. Glenda said three was tops.

She gave me a plate with three winkeyes to carry and I did, over to the table we had that tilted real easy, tilted enough to slop cereal from a bowl, but would not tilt over. I held the table steady with a toe and sicced my hunger quick after that stack of winkeyes.

Basil slouched against the fridge, scratching his toothbrush at his teeth, and ran his mouth about a silly story he had already unloaded on us once that morning.

"Anyhow, the boy gets naked and humps his young ass up the tree trunk to where the cute knothole is, talks sweet and pokes it . . ."

"Then he slips, don't he?"

". . . snaps his dick like a pretzel."

"Takes two doctors to rig him a dick-splint from Popsicle sticks."

"The boy says, 'That maple is a sneaky, no-good bitch!'"

They giggled crazy at that, giggled like a big bag of giggles had busted open.

Glenda sat across the tilting table from me and had her own regular breakfast of java and smokes and stray bites from my plate. She never did look worse than okay, and that morn in bed clothes with a sleepy face she did look way better than that.

She spoke low to me. "Eat up and get outside, Shug. Who knows what the hell'll happen in here—understand?"

I nodded and she nodded.

"You get on outside and mow the bone orchard."

"I will."

"I never can get that ol' tractor to run the way you can, Shug. You've got the knack."

"Mom, I'll do it."

For some short minutes I sat facedown and stared at the empty plate. I put spit on a fingertip and stabbed crumbs that stuck in the spit, then raised the finger and licked the crumbs clean.

Smoke rose from Glenda and each new big noise caused her eyes to flinch and she would pull her nightclothes together tighter at the throat.

"Better get," she said. "He's boiled."

I ran to the john. I had business there.

When I came back to the kitchen Red stood before Glenda, saying, "I don't know for how long, but we're goin' out scallybippin'. You got that now?"

"Bring plenty of shit," Basil said.

"There's two bottles over there."

"I *do* feel like drivin' some. You know how I get, I get to feel like drivin', drivin', drivin'."

Then Glenda said, "There's not a dollar in the house, Red."

"Poor baby."

"There's maybe fifty cents somewhere."

"Aw! That won't buy you no bus ticket to nowhere, huh, honey?"

"I'm thinkin' food, Red. I'm thinkin' breakfast, lunch, and supper. I'm thinkin' about soap powder so your clothes are clean. I'm thinkin' . . ."

"Quit! Quit thinkin' and tellin' me about it." Red plumbed deep in his jeans pocket and raised his fist around a choker of cash, then unleashed a long jerky sweep of his arm and threw the cash like dice onto the table. The choker of cash stopped rolling smack under her nose. "Now you best hush the fuck up about what you think."

I pushed out the screen door to the back stoop, then moved towards the shed. A wave of goldfinches rolled from a tree as I passed and rolled away towards the sun. A train screamed over the hill. I could see out into the bone orchard and could see two ladies there who stood holding hands beside a grave so fresh it was just raw dirt in a heap. They did drop flowers on the dirt.

The tractor shed leaned some, an old shed of gray wood leaning some, and it had junk written on the inside walls by ink pens and crayons that went back to at least "Ozark League Champions 1938." Some of the written stuff came across funny but most seemed to be by people pining for people they ain't going to know the way they want.

The tractor started up with the first touch and I backed into the side yard.

The back door to the house swung open and Red and Basil came out. Red wore a stag-cut black shirt that left his big arms of big muscles on view, and he'd done a recent slicking of his hair. Red was coming to me. Basil climbed behind the wheel of the car he drove that day, a tan Impala I admired, and fired the engine. I sat upon the tractor seat and saw that Red had something to say. He wiggled his fingers in that way of wiggling that means come closer. I leaned down closer to him and got my ear to his mouth.

"Keep an eye on that witch, dig?"

EXCEPT for the noise of the tractor it rode about the way I figured some horses might. Except also for the stink of oil smoke and gas and the noise when the gears gnashed. Except for all that it rode pretty horsey, jostly and bouncy, me sitting high in the saddle wearing spurs. The exhaust smoke would remind me by the minute though that I rode not an Appaloosa named Tango or Champ, but an old gas-burner that did not prance and did not cut much of a figure, but did get the job done.

The grass had sprung a little too high to where it rippled in the wind, and Mr. Goynes, who checked the grounds on days I didn't see coming, liked the grass short and stiff and never rippling. To do the grass used four hours as a rule. The tractor part took ninety minutes and the other minutes got used pushing the regular mower in the tighter spots, and mowing those tighter spots caused the minutes that made the job sweaty and in some heats awful.

The cemetery offered more than one look, more than one feel. The tombstones came in a variety of ways. The oldest needed to be read with fingers, the words and numbers had been blown off by the years and the stuff years throw at a thing, so the names were only a letter here and a letter there, though the rock still stood. In the newer parts the tombstones tended to shine and stand clean and easy to read as a stop sign. There were lots of names hammered into those tombstones of all ages that had the same names as many of the streets of town that I would walk on when I went around. Same names as streets and stores and car lots and grade schools. I shaved the fuzz from the entire dead, one and all, if I ever had heard of them, or never had, I gave the same shave to each.

A church group of boys and girls passed along the road beside the bone orchard, hiking over the hill to Hudkins Park or maybe doing the long hike clear out to Canaday Bridge. The girls mostly wore shorts and several held long sticks while they hiked. Their legs flashed by in the sun like spokes. The boys walked at the back and walked like they were by themselves. There were plenty in the church group who knew me, and me them, but none did wave, so me neither.

In the last hour of mowing Glenda came out and came over to me. She brought me a giant glass of cola. She had a dress on, the summer kind with flowers in the cloth, and I swelled looking at how good she looked, Glenda. Her face had eased of nerves and fear and her hair was combed loose.

My lips made a dive for the cola the way pony lips dive for a pond.

"I think he was so messed in the head he grabbed out of the wrong pocket, Shug. He left a fair little pile. More'n he knew, I expect. And you know what that makes me think? That makes me think a boy who works as hard as you deserves to see a movie tonight. You think you'd like to take me to a movie tonight? Would you?"

GRANNY Akins could not chew much. Not too many teeth stuck in her head and none of the best teeth did. She was sickly skinny and might have been sickly skinny even with teeth. Her hair was some shade of white, but not pure. Her skin looked like a dry leaf fallen to the road and waiting to crinkle into pieces. She had the little-bitty Akins place outside the city limits and lived in it off government checks and her paper route, a route I helped her throw once in a while, especially in winter.

She stopped by after pitching her papers that time and came in and sat a spell. She did say she had news, but did not share it for about three cigarettes and a tumbler of Glenda's tea. Granny was also fond of regular sips from the stuff in Glenda's tea but never bothered to claim it was tea she sipped.

"Carl's comin' on home," she said. "He'll get partway on a airplane first, then ride a bus."

I asked, "Is he . . . ?"

"He ain't sayin', boy. Not yet."

"Well, still—I can't wait! Carl likes stuff I like!"

Uncle Carl was Red's surprise baby brother but had first been a surprise baby to Granny who had reckoned her body too old for hatching babies. Carl came along eighteen years junior to Red and had got himself scrambled with the Marines during the springtime past. We each, even Red, had watched the news hard for news of Carl's squad until the telegram came that said he was hurt for good and gone from there. He had been for quite a while in a hospital with a Mexican sort of name waiting to find out if he would have to hop places the rest of his life or could he learn to walk okay again.

"We'll sure be glad to see him," Glenda said. "I hope it didn't get his face."

"He ain't said that it did."

"Boy, I can't wait to see Carl."

"I needed to come by to tell Red, but naturally he's off somewheres."

"I'll be sure and tell him," Glenda said. "He might be out a week—who knows."

"Not me," Granny said. "I never did know."

Supper cooked on the stove. The smell had grown strong and smelled ready to be dished. I knew and Glenda knew that Granny felt bad eating in front of people, any people, even kin, but Glenda had to say something.

"Would you eat, Granny?"

"Oh, no, no," she said, and stood up with her head shaking. "No, I believe I eat best on what I cook myself. My diet, you understand. My diet which I need to run along home and fix. Y'all just let Red know what I told you. The grass out there sure does look fine, Shug."

WHEN the doors to the movie house flung open Glenda and me were carried out by the crowd. The crowd rushed us along caught between all those other people, bumped about and carried away like the chuck wagon amidst a cow stampede. This stampede here was only a short one and ended when folks spilled their different ways in the parking lot. The lot was new the same as the movie house, and topped by whitish gravel. The gravel showed well in the night. Dust lay beneath the gravel and cars took off fast and did kick the dust into the air and the dust rose in spurts behind wheels and stirred a boiling cloud, then settled.

"Shug, wasn't that girl behind us a girl you know?"

"She was in my grade, is all."

"I believe, li'l sweet mister, that she was trying to get you to notice her."

"I saw her."

"When girls get moony about you, hon, you should be friendly back."

"Girls don't get moony about me. Plus, I don't care."

"She was squirmin' like she liked you."

"Probably she had to pee and didn't want to miss any movie."

Glenda had dressed herself nice in a light-red dress and tall white shoes and had her raven hair covered by a red scarf. Men surely did take looks at her. When she walked she got that meat to shaking awful pretty on her bones. It was the sort of shaking that did appeal to most. Most would look, some would look away real sudden and clinch their gals, and plenty made whistle-lips and gestures that go with whistle-lips.

The car Red had left behind was a Dodge. The Dodge was blue on the body, white on top. The Dodge was by years not all that old, but it had turned a high total of miles in those years and was not going to stand for too much more.

When we got to the car Glenda just stood there, so I stood there, too, watching her. She smelled of tea, but I dug the smell of tea on her.

"Well?" she went. "Well?"

"I don't know," I said. "Well, what?"

"Get the *door* for me, Shug. You hold the door for *ladies*."

"Oh."

"Didn't you notice the man in the movie?"

"Uh-huh." I pulled the door open and held it wide for her. "But he was, uh, like a rich, rich man—I *knew* those types did this shit."

"You should, too, Shug."

I went around and got in, slid into the passenger seat, and she had her cigarette pack in her hand and again went, "Well?"

I remembered this part from the movie. Her lighter was on the seat. I took the pack from her, shook two smokes loose, stuck them in my mouth and scratched a flame from the lighter. I puffed and puffed to get both smokes burning good, then handed one to her.

I said, "There you are, madam."

Glenda liked that. She grinned and snickered.

"Shall we go?" she said.

The Dodge had that row of buttons on the dash where you pushed a button to change gears on the car. That style of shifting gears seemed funny to us both. She took the first hill slow, then swung onto a dirt road that would make for a roundabout back way to the house. She goosed the gas then and her scarf flapped and snapped in the wind. The dirt road had ruts across it but she kept the gas pedal down, so some ruts we hit and bounced, but there were plenty we sailed over smooth, too.

"I'm gonna stop here, hon. I like the man to drive."

"You mean it?"

"Get behind the wheel and see."

I got out and went around and she slid over to let me take the wheel.

"I punch D, right?"

"Mm-hmm."

I just could reach the gas pedal good. I did not steer us too straight but I did miss the ditches on either side. Glenda poured herself some tea, shook fresh smokes from the pack for her and me, then handed me mine burning. I clenched it with the hand high on the steering wheel. I guess I drove slow, too slow, and seemed a boy, a boring boy driver.

Glenda eased over and sat where a date sits when her boyfriend is at the wheel. She scooted in snug to me. She put an arm across my shoulders. She kissed me on the cheek, mainly, but touching the mouth.

"Faster wouldn't scare me, hon."

I did okay going faster on the dirt road. Glenda laughed and squeezed my neck. I got up to a fair speed. Rocks kicked about under the car and made pings and thuds. She laid kisses on me a few times. Curves I took fine but full turns tested my steering. When we came to the main road, the hard road into town that ran to the bone orchard, I took it too fast and leaked wide in the turn, nearly to the far curb, then pulled on the wheel too hard the other way. Glenda slapped a hand on the wheel to help me get straight. We both had begun laughs of relief before the bubble lights of a cop flashed behind us.

"Oops!" went Glenda. "Stay cool."

"What do I do?"

"Don't stop. Not yet. Don't stop 'til you get in our drive."

Home was straight down the road. It took a minute more of steering, which went okay except when a car came at me and the car had big headlights aimed in my eyes. Glenda muttered something but not about my steering. I closed my eyes to the blinding lights and my body went still like I was trying to keep my balance like I thought keeping my balance would keep the car straight on the road.

The bubble lights behind didn't mess me up.

The drive had been laid out to be maybe one hundred yards long, and curled. The drive ran through the heart of the bone orchard and had two clear ruts and a little stripe of regular dirt and grass ran between the ruts. The cop followed us right onto the drive and on up to the front of the house.

Glenda said, "Don't say a thing."

"Mom—the lights are on inside the house!"

"Oh, crap," she said. "Hit P for park."

The cop had got out of his car and had come to stand by ours by the time we got out. He was a cop from town who looked familiar. He'd been by before.

He said, "What the hell was that back there at the corner?"

Glenda said, "I dropped my cigarette and lost concentration for only that one second or two. Silly ol' me."

"Uh-huh. But since the boy there was drivin', that

ain't gonna work for an excuse."

"What do you mean, the boy was drivin'? Huh? That's *crazy*."

"Mrs. Akins—don't. You can put all the wings you want on that dog but it still ain't goin' to fly. I seen the boy drivin', and that's for certain."

"Oh, phooey," she went. "I let Shug drive the last little bit home 'cause he has got to learn somehow. Isn't that a fact? Boys have to learn *some*-how."

"Have you been drinkin'?"

"Not especially."

The front house door was open to the screen and I saw Red ease up to where he could see and hear, then pretty quick he shoved out.

He said, "Is that you, Herren?"

"Hello, Red. You been bein' good?"

"Yup. What's your problem with my wife?" Red came down the steps, no shirt on but his hair combed, and he had that calm way about him that I'd seen before and my legs got jittery. My heart revved high seeing him seeming so calm. He put his hands on his hips and tried to smile. "She didn't mean nothin'."

"She can go," Herren said. "Just, I don't want to see nothin' like that again. That sound fair, ma'am?"

She said, "That's a mighty fancy mustache you got."

"Thanks, ma'am, it catches crumbs real good."

Me and Glenda made it to the porch and stood there and kept touching our hands to each other.

"Is your parole up?"

"This fall."

"You workin'?"

"Odd-job sort of stuff, 'round and about."

Glenda did take me by the hand about then, and lead me up the few steps of the porch and into the front room. I could hear fingernails tapping on the sink in the kitchen. The tapping sounds did sound upset.

She said, "I'm afraid we stepped in it but good."

The cop car soon headed away and Red came inside. He turned at the screen door and watched until the cop had gone from sight.

"He's out of here," he said.

"Good," Glenda said. "He seemed nice."

"Did he?" Red hit her flush just above her left eye. The scarf flew back and fell around her neck. She bent in half and spun away. He punched her in the back, grabbed her hair and jerked until her face pulled clear of her hands, and smacked her more, whipping her to and fro with his fingers spread, numerous sharp bony smacks. "You just nearly got that 'nice' cop killed, you know that? I *ain't takin'* another fall—so I'd've had to take fuckin' *Herren* off the fuckin' count, dig?"

"Let her be," I said, which I knew not to say, I knew not to speak up to him, not ever, but then I did. "*I was drivin'.*"

Red had all the bad habits but still did seem a good athlete. He made moves as fast as a housefly moves. He hit me in the gut with a punch that dropped me towards the floor but did also manage to clout the back of my head before I reached bottom.

"You punched him! Damn you!" Glenda raised her hands so her fingernails might save her, but Red grabbed her by both wrists and shook and shook her.

"Come here! Come here, you witch! You, too, fat boy."

I had spread a thick spittle of supper on the rug.

He raised me by the neck and drug us to the kitchen, where he screamed, "*Never* draw no fuckin' heat on me! Are you idiots?"

The kitchen was stacked full with swag. The swag was soda, soda bottles in wooden cases, and the wooden cases stood in stacks from wall to wall in the kitchen. The back door could hardly be got to. The overhead light was blocked by an eclipse of swag. This swag amounted to around two hundred cases of soda, I would imagine, and several crates of other items with a value I could not guess.

Basil stood next to the sink in a slump. Basil never liked to be around this side of Red. He did not care to be on hand whenever Red led a family boil-over.

He said, "This'll be out of your kitchen tomorrow night, Glenda. There's a guy who'll take all we got."

"Don't tell her nothin'—she might let slip to the *nice* cop."

Her eye was rising, just at the eyebrow, even in the bad light flesh rose so I could see a blood egg rising, and as it rose it pulled the skin so her eye took on a sorry lumped shape. Her nose was walloped an ugly kind of rosy and her top lip swollen, but no blood spilled that I saw. She did try not to cry but could not keep a few leaks from running.

A strange something had happened to me that night and I looked off from her swelling and trying not to cry and let myself loose at him. I came loose from sense and did try to rush the man, but he pushed me hard to the floor and laughed.

"I would've slapped you, boy, but shit splatters."

She took a swipe at him and he clamped claws on her nipples, clamped truly mean, and twisted until she sagged and moaned and fell away snuffling.

I rushed him again. He shoved me up against the fridge easy as tossing a pillow. I raised my hands as fists, trembling fists. The stacks of swag seemed to be taking his side, edging close, backing him up.

"Oh yeah, baby! You're thinkin' of hittin' me now, ain't you, fat boy? Think you've got to where you're ready? Huh?" Each time he said huh he smacked my head backwards so it thumped the icebox door. "Huh? Huh? Huh? Huh? Oh yeah, baby, you want to hit me! Hit Daddy! Huh? Come on with it, boy. Hit Daddy! I mean it, come on. Huh? Don't want to? Huh? Got your dukes ready, boy, so swing at me. Come on, come on. Huh? Huh?"

"Ol' son, ol' son," said Basil. "Don't bust him up to where we can't use the kid. Don't bust him up—we'll be soon needin' the kid."

"Did I fuckin' ask you? Did I?"

Basil held his hands up in surrender.

"Now, don't bother whippin' me, Red—I'm already whipped. Remember? I came in here whipped. No need to whip me."

"Aw, man," went Red. "Aw, man—let's split."

"There's a notion."

"Let's split and run wild."

"I'm sold, ol' son."

Red turned to Glenda. He breathed real fierce so his nostrils flexed and his lips curled like he wanted to spit some shit he'd been waiting all his life to spit in her face. She did not raise her face to him.

"Listen here—I'm goin' out now, see, and I'm goin' out to *bag my limit*. So fuck you. And your fat boy? That tub of shit ain't never goin' to get to no age, *ever*, where he wants to mess with me, dig? The day ain't goin' to come when he can whip me for you. Not now, not ever. So fuck the both of you."

She and me slumped to the floor there and sat breathing hard. The bad light helped us not to look at each other just yet. We heard the screen door slam. I hated him solid that night. We heard car doors slam. Her dress had lost two buttons. We heard the engine roar and the car rattle away down the drive.

"I guess I'll fetch ice," I said. "If there is any."

"No, no, hon—you sit. I'll fetch the ice. You just sit. Mom'll fetch the ice this time."

6

THE NEXT PLACE WAS A HOUSE. Wherever dope beckoned from I would be sent. The house was part of a nest of houses down the highway, a village called Wamper, and hung back from the street it was on. The path to the house from the street called for sixty paces, easy. The house had been made of bricks, with two levels, and a yard lamp in front and a pretty rock patio to the side that also included a brick barbecue pit. Old trees laid out plenty of shade and the yard did also have flowers showing bright colors along the edges.

"You just walk on in like you belong there," Red said. "Walk in like you're best buddies with the kid that lives there."

"*He'll* be there, though."

"He's sick. He ain't goin' to say much to you, and even if he did say somethin' he can't *do* nothin'. He's *sick*."

"That's the whole deal," Basil said. "The kid's sick, Shug, so you want to get in there quick before he uses all them painkillers they give him. Find what gives him relief and steal it."

I don't guess I said anything to that.

Red looked at his sheet of paper that had addresses and other news typed up and down on it.

"Patty reckons there should be plenty, too. They just checked the kid out last night."

Basil drove back and forth twice so I could see the

house and the way to it and the ways to get inside it and set the map in my mind. Not far along the street, neighbor kids played army in the woods that grew beside a puny creek that cut between houses. They carried those play rifles that spouted corks and play hand-grenades and were busy laying ambushes in the weeds for each other and did not see us pass. That day the car was still the tan Impala I dug, and Basil had tried to get me jolly and josh me along on this errand by driving fast, making the engine growl, showing me how to speed-shift from second gear to fourth, until Red said, "That's right, dipshit, get us pulled over on our way to steal dope so the fuzz'll know *for a fact* we were around here."

On past the creek and the kids playing war, Basil turned around, faced again towards the brick house, and put the Impala at idle. I could see those kids in the weeds, flat on the ground, about to spring a trap on the kids that were shuffling along on patrol. Past them I saw a yellow car pull from the drive at the brick house. It came towards us.

"Put your head down. Heads down. . . . Okay, it's gone." Red jerked me close to him as he could. "Listen, if you get jumped up in there, and maybe you could punch or kick some and get away, then okay, go ahead. But don't stab nobody or nothin' crazy."

"I won't."

"You don't need to," Basil said. "You don't need to be stabbin' over a B-and-E charge, not at your age."

"Don't hit 'em in the head with a brick or nothin', neither—you never do know with that stuff, see, how the skull will take it, and you got no priors."

"*Plus* you're a juvie."

"You won't get much but maybe a mean talkin'-to. They'll talk mean and try to throw a scare at you and see if it sticks."

"I don't know about this," I said. "I don't feel so hot."

"Bullshit, bullshit," went Red. "Bull-shit."

"Loosen your wig, Shug. Really. This ain't no biggie."

"And get goin'. Get out, and get your flabby ass goin'."

They gave me a satchel to tote. The satchel had a strap that hooked over my shoulder, and the pouch part said on the side "Grit." This would make me seem to be out selling *Grit*, that country sort of newspaper containing many country sayings and farmer facts and such, door to door. I made the satchel into saddlebags in my thoughts. My horse had broke a leg in the desert but the gold dust remained in the saddlebags. I walked on out of the desert in the blazing sun and past the soldiers in the creek and the couple of houses between the creek and the brick house.

A cat sat stretching in the yard and looked at me and said something. Its mouth opened showing pink and a noise came loose. I nodded, Howdy, cat. The big shade from the old trees felt sweet to walk under. I had a strong sweat running and the shade fell over me feeling the good way a surprise breeze feels.

A black motor scooter leaned against the side of the brick house, beside the paved drive, the sort of scooter you stand on and has a horn that makes yips instead of honks. Back next to the garage the nose of a white boat poked out from below a green tarp, and another cat rested in the shadow under the boat. The barbecue pit let out a smell from meat drippings burned and sauce scorched during family get-togethers, a sort of happy-ashes smell.

The side door was not locked. The hinges squeaked forth a sound of croaking, a long yawning croak.

"*Grit?*" I said, like I hoped nobody would hear. "*Grit* for sale.*"

That door yawned open to let me into the kitchen. The kitchen was spick-and-span, all in order, kept cleaner than my ears. Jugs and canisters and a bread box sat on the counter to hold stuff from sight. A cuckoo clock did tick-tick-tick high on a wall. An open doorway took me into another room where a jumbo table of wood stood, and the wood glowed from polish, surrounded by chairs that matched the wood and the glow. A bunch of doilies, a white kind, were spread about on the table, but spread about on purpose, spread to spots they were meant to rest on.

All kinds of nice things showed themselves in that house. I figured I knew from TV shows that in a house of this nature the kid would have his own room upstairs, maybe even with a separate john. Thick carpet covered the steps on the stairs. The rail was wooden and thick, with tracks and grooves running up it in a design I did not get but thought handsome. The stairs elbowed left halfway up.

At the top step I heard the kid breathing. His breaths

came with a crumpling quality at the edge, like his breaths were wadded first, then choked down. The breaths sounded at a steady slow pace and pulled me straight to the sick kid, who was a bald teenager, I imagine, with skin the color of fog, taking breaths he had to crumple and wad to swallow. His bed had got rich with pillows but he did use just two, both plumped behind him with the others tossed around the bed.

The pills, and the other stuff, the liquid stuff, sat on a side table in plain sight. I went directly to them and stood between the dope and the sick kid. He had an airplane on a string dangling from the ceiling near a corner, the two-winged style of plane. He had his own TV over on top of a chest of drawers. A trio of ribbons that are given out as awards for various good activities hung from tacks or some such beside a wall mirror that had photos wedged into the frame.

The sick kid I think knew I stood there. His bald head, way bald, would move a little, and his eyes would roll open and point at me, see me and stay on me, then the awakeness would sink away from his eyes and they would be on me still but not seeing me, then fall shut. I picked up the pills and gave the bottle a shake and here came those eyes again, those big sick eyes set in that way bald head, then the awakeness sinking and the eyes falling shut and those breaths he fought so hard to swallow.

I tapped four pills from the bottle and laid them in clear view on the side table, but I had to be sure Red got plenty. I guess I did then take the rest of the doctor-ordered dope, did take it all, pill and liquid, and stuffed the *Grit* satchel.

After I walked most of the paces down the drive that yellow car pulled in and rolled up to me and paused. The mother, I suppose, with a bottle of milk and whatnot in a grocery sack beside her. Her window was down and I spoke first, "*Grit*, ma'am?"

"We don't take *Grit*."

"That's okay," I said. "I've sold quite a few."

"Your day is made," she said, and let up on the brake and rolled to near the side door.

I don't know if she looked or did not look, but I know I ran. My legs made the choice more than my head and I did beat feet and beat hard out into the street, past the creek and those kids in the weeds at war, racing to the tan Impala.

"Don't run!" Red said. He said that as I jumped inside the car. "Don't run—unless somebody's right behind you. Is somebody right behind you?"

"Might be," I said. I was in a stage of melting down, sweat gushing. "The mother came home."

Basil gunned the engine and took us away from there at a welcome rate of speed. He raced us down the hard road with tires squealing, then ducked us away on a dirt backroad nobody looking would look for us on.

"Now, if somebody's right behind you, then of course you run, dig?"

"Run like hell, too."

"Otherwise, don't run."

"I ain't feelin' too good."

"Don't be a puss. It's just the jitters nippin' at you, fat

boy. Grab you a beer there and kick on back. We done got the goodies, and we done got gone, too."

THE sheet of paper Red carried said the next errand should be run at this house in West Table, a scrunched small white place with many vines clung to the walls, over near the city park. When I walked up the footpath to the house I could smell full ashtrays through a screen window. I could hear the noise of somebody sleeping a sleep that was not smooth, but a sleep that contained hemming and hawing and sputters.

The second door to this house set clear around to the back. I toted the *Grit* satchel and walked in like I had heard a voice invite me inside to make a sale. The first room was the mud room, a tight area where garden tools and muddy galoshes were kept. Then came the kitchen. This kitchen was of the sort I had experienced and the implements and foods and odors there did not stump me as to what was what. A block of frozen meat sat on the sideboard thawing, pork, I believe.

The sleeping sounds guided me. The sick person at this house had been laid down in the parlor. A bed looked wrong in that room but that is where it had been put. This sick person seemed to be a very very old man who I'd guess was shrinking fast. His skin wrapped loose around him. The hair had also been culled from his head, and the skin lay pale and thin on his skull so that I could see the veins clear as cracks in a windshield.

A table near his head had a lamp on it and tissues, and all kinds of medical dope assembled there.

My thought then went: Tough in the morning, tough 'til lights-out.

His eyes opened sudden, and he said, "No game today, Bill?"

"Uh—we won," I said. "Purty easy."

"It's good of you to leave harvest and be here."

"No sweat."

"I've somehow got on the wrong ship."

"You sure about that?"

"I'm on the wrong ship. The wrong ship. No game, Bill?"

A voice behind me shocked me silly, saying, "Go on and speak up to him, boy. Speak up."

The voice went with a tiny delicate old white-haired lady.

"I heard him through the window, and thought he called me, ma'am," I said. "He thinks I'm somebody else, that must be why he called me."

"It ain't the first time," she said. "It ain't the second or third, neither. Bill was his brother."

"Just like in Japan," the man said. "Get a stout 'un, Bill."

"Tell him you're Bill—he's been callin' for Bill all day."

"*This is Bill*," I said, sort of loud. "I think we're on the right ship now."

"I felt I'd got on the wrong ship."

"Naw, listen, *this is Bill*—it's the right ship."

I don't know what he thought of what I told him but his eyes closed.

"He might sleep," she said. She looked me up and

down, then smiled. "Would you eat a cookie?"

"I could."

"Come to the kitchen."

She led away from the parlor, and I spun to the dope there on the table, then did a swift rake of all the bottles and such, a swift rake of dope into the *Grit* satchel. The satchel tinkled.

The cookies were oatmeal with raisins and I stuffed down three or four in a short time. She offered more.

"I've got to get," I said. "Papers to sell."

"I'd take a *Grit* from you, boy. You're such a nice boy to play along with him."

The sick man began then to call for Caleb, asking if Caleb was here, where is Caleb, oh, Caleb.

She said, "I don't know who that Caleb is he calls for. That one's a puzzle. I don't recall *any* Caleb."

"I could be Caleb, too," I said. "I'll step back there just a minute."

"That'd be nice if you would."

I returned to stand beside the sick person.

"Caleb got here," I said. "He's on the right ship with you."

"It's the wrong ship, wrong, wrong."

I opened a couple of the pill bottles and shook piles of the pills onto the table. They rattled a good deal.

"Who is that?" he said.

"Caleb and Bill are on the ship." I looked at the other bottles in the satchel and could not say what they were, but I made a guess and set one down and left it there and hoped it was the bottle he would need most.

"Is it you?"

"Yeah, it's me."

As I passed through the kitchen the old lady reached for my arm and said, "I'd take that *Grit* now."

"Oh. Geez. I'll have to run to the boss's stack and fetch more. I ran out. Wait for me, would you? I'll be back in a jiffy."

MY heart took to hopping so it bounced against my teeth. I waited to be found out. By the sun it was time to eat, but Basil kept driving in circles to nowhere special, and Red kept looking into the Grit satchel. I waited to be beat when I was found out. The dope I had snatched from the old man amounted to a letdown for Red. Him and Basil were high on tastes of the dope from the brick house, plus beer they pulled from a sack, and kept looking at me, baffled.

"They don't seem to pack these bottles full as they should," Red said. "There's lots of air in there."

Basil said, "That's how them doctors can go skiing and good stuff like that. Visit Hawaii."

"Heaven help that old man," Red said, "'cause he's been kickin' the gong around *real heavy* in there. Dig this, Basil—there ain't but nine reds, here, and half a bottle of punch."

"No shit? Whew, but would I like to be as fucked up as he must be about now."

"I took what was there," I said. "An old woman was home, too, you know."

"Think she's been poppin' some?"

"*No!*"

"What're you drivin' at, then?"

"Maybe she hides some. From *him*."

"Huh. I guess that could be."

My gut gave out wiry, boing-boing noises by the time Basil pulled into a driveway a block from the town square. The house there was a shotgun shack, but not run down to junk yet. Paint hadn't chipped too bad, and the porch did not sag. There were lawn chairs on the dirt yard, and a Ford Fairlane was parked in front of us. A woman in a white uniform and soft white shoes came to the door, then waved to us.

"She's home," said Red. "Let's visit."

She came out to meet us, and her and Red kissed. On the mouth. Kissed on the mouth, and he patted her butt, and she clung to his neck and I saw their tongues touch.

"I'll bet you've been busy," she said. She stood taller than Red. Her hair was plain ol' everyday brown and wrapped in a knot. "I'll bet you've brung over somethin' good."

"Yes, ma'am, the wingding may now start."

"By y'all's eyes I'd say the wingding started a while ago."

"Just layin' a base, Patty," Basil said. He wore a grin that did not seem to be grinned over any certain thing. "Somethin' to build on."

Other people were inside the house. A radio was turned on, news, or something that was just talk. Basil sat on a lawn chair and popped a beer. Red and her went at it some more, mewing and grabbing.

All I did was stand there.

Patty looked like a bug bite compared to Glenda.

They got awful familiar in front of me. When they broke from their clinch Red called me to him with a hand wave.

"Here's a couple of bucks, boy." I took the money he gave and it was as he said, exactly a couple of bucks. "You need to scoot yourself on home. Grown-up shit's liable to happen."

"Okay."

"Yeah, and listen here—what is it we done today?"

"Men stuff?"

"Good for you, you got it." He patted my back as if he did not know I hated him. "Now beat it, boy. Scoot back to the house."

7

CARL'S BAD LEG LOOKED LIKE a sausage link that had got shoved to the back of the fridge and forgot about 'til it was no good. The leg had lost a chunk down low, in the calf part, and seemed withery above and below the crater left where the chunk belonged. The crater skin had a deep darkness. The withery skin looked to be a solid scar. The leg was withery with a chunk gone but did still move, it did move but not too good, so Carl hopped some when he walked.

"Pogey bait," he said, answering a kid question I had put to him. "Candy was called pogey bait."

"Huh. Like, 'Let's eat pogey bait'?"

"Aye, aye."

Me and Glenda had drove out to see him at the Akins place and the heat chased us into the yard under the shade trees. The house there was tiny to where two or three the same size could be stuffed inside a real house. I do not know who built a house to be that tiny size. The roof was shingled by gray tar shingles and the walls were shingled the same. Several items that did not work anymore rusted or rotted here or there in the yard and five loose chickens murmured and pecked at the dirt. Bare dirt patches showed between grassy places in the yard and if wind came along the grass would ripple.

Glenda said, "I am sure you'll heal fine, just fine."

"That makes one of us."

Carl sat on a wood chair leaned against a mimosa

tree, drinking beer, wearing green Marine Corps pants with the cloth of one leg cut away so the messed-up leg hung out in the open air. His skin had picked up a yellow tint from a bug he had caught that got in his blood and spread that color, especially to his face. The yellow tint made his eyes seem bluer. His hair was blond to the edge of white. He did not wear a shirt and had become thin. The dog tags for when you're killed and they need to know the name of your body dangled shiny to his chest. He smoked many many no-filter cigarettes. On the dirt next to his chair he had started stacking empty beer cans, arranging them to stand just so, trying, I imagine, to build himself a tall welcome-home stack of empties.

I asked, "What was it like?"

"You'll find out."

"I will? When?"

"When they send *you*."

Glenda and me sat there on the grass near him and she looked shook by his wounds, shook hard and made sad. The lump over her eye had sunk back flat but wrong colors showed yet along her brow. I could tell she might weep. She poured and poured from her silvery thermos. When she tossed back tea she turned her face sideways towards the woods. The woods squeezed close at the very edge of the yard on three sides and stood there glum like a crowd that had patience and more patience but was not so sure they ever would be entertained.

Glenda said, "I'll pitch in to help Granny with the food, I guess. It ought to be near ready."

The heat made eyes droop even in the shade. I fell back slow and looked up. The pink parts of the mimosa called out to hummingbirds, called out something good, and a pair of hummers went ffft! ffft! from one pink part to the next, stabbing their noses in, draining the juice. All the way up past the limbs through the tree and into the sky, far up into the blue, a hawk prowled on the hot breezes, wings held wide and stiff, prowling in a silent circle for creatures of the type it liked to kill.

I heard Glenda and Granny fussing about salt.

I sat up and Carl had a smoke going and was leaned sideways adding another empty to his stack. A pyramid, I think. His fingers worked calm and steady.

"You reckon you'll still like giggin' frogs and all that stuff?"

"If there's a pond I can get to, I will."

"Hell, I know plenty, Carl."

"Do you? That's bad fuckin' news for frogs then, ain't it?"

The food came out of the house in a black kettle. Glenda carried the kettle. The food was what Carl favored and had missed: navy beans and ham over cornbread with a squirt of hot sauce. Granny followed along behind Glenda, bringing cornbread, bowls, and spoons. She walked in that very careful way she did walk when a little bit drunk. Both of them appeared to be softened and made moist by the heat in that tiny kitchen with the oven on.

"Start shovelin' it," Granny said. Her words wobbled loose from her mouth with so few teeth to cut edges on them. Sometimes her words only came kind of close to sounding like what she wanted to say. "There's gobs and gobs to eat, so y'all pull your spoons and start to shovelin'."

THE chickens bounced up from the dirt when we pegged beans at them. Their heads jerked and their feathers fluffed as they bounced and their claws paddled frantic in the air. Spoons worked nice to flip the beans. Carl would say, "Incoming!" and me and him would pull back on our spoons loaded with beans and peg the chickens. We kept them bouncing. The chickens bounced and seemed to become things of a different shape in the air, suddenly puffy and fattened scared things, and they came down with their legs running hard before they hit ground and their heads spun like their necks were rubber bands, but they did not cluck off out of range. They acted the way cartoons act. Cartoons you could smell, and peg with beans.

"Glad you'ns're enjoyin' them beans," Granny said. She had stretched out on a white blanket in shade next to Glenda, and did seem drunk. "Does good for my heart seein' how you 'preciate them beans, son."

"Yup," Carl said. He held his bowl in his lap, and for a spell stared down at the leavings, the few white beans and dried juice. Then he spoke, the words coming with spaces between them. "Funny . . . what you . . . *think* . . . you miss."

"I don't expect I'd miss beans," I said. "Ice cream—I could see missin' that. Winkeyes."

"You don't know what you'd miss, Shug." An airplane, the passenger kind, passed overhead, a silver dot high in the blue, and made that sad sound in the sky, that sort of sad hum from a thing far away and going farther that makes your chest leak air and feel hollow. "It might be candy corn, or maybe matchbooks from the pancake house that you'd have in your head all the time. Some silly thing your head decides is important and misses. A picture of your dog. Your old baseball mitt. There's no knowin' which silly thing, neither. Not before it happens."

The sun had gone out west, and sunlight came back our way at a slant and threw shadows that stretched longer. Slanted light and long shadows and the gurgle of a beer can draining. Little poot-poot sounds did also occur, poot-poot sounds Glenda made dozing on the white blanket in the long shadows.

Glenda wore jeans washed pale and her legs flopped apart in a V as she dozed, and the pale jeans rode up her ankles some, laying her white white skin out open to the air.

In sleep she had often shoved her way into my dreams and got in there and set me dreaming weird pictures during plenty of nighttimes. The weird dreams happened elsewhere, elsewhere from places I knew. I guess most dreams happened near the equator because Glenda was dressed for heat in each and every one. She loped across acres of sand wearing little pieces of cloth and got girly-girl in the short water, kicking her feet the way she did, tossing off big grins and wild laughs. I was somewhere behind her, usually. Somewhere behind but close behind. Coconuts and bananas and foods such as that were littered about and easy to get. She jumped around and cut up on the sand, kicking in the short water, dressed for heat, giving me impressions that saddled good feelings on me that rode my thoughts past the end of the dreams and on into the true bullshit of the next day.

Sometimes she swam in the waves naked but never would leave the water.

"Say, listen here, Shug—why don't you throw your feet thataway towards the house there, then fetch 'em back *thisaway* carryin' me a couple more beers, huh? In fact, let's make that a order."

I did do the order. Not so many beers were left if his thirst hung on. I fetched back the two cold beers he ordered me after, and while I did that Basil spun from the rock road and into the drive. This was some other car he drove. A Mercury of such size people called them battleships. They often *would* waddle like an ocean rolled under them. This one was a wore-out black color. Red's cowboy boots dangled from a back window, and Basil wheeled on past the Dodge and Granny's rattly Ford wagon in the drive and onto the yard, coming to where we sat. The tires crunching across the yard and the bellowing engine flushed the chickens towards the woods, then the Mercury skidded to a stop a foot or two shy of the mimosa tree.

Basil came springing from the battleship grinning, his fine white teeth on parade, and came quick over to Carl and kissed the crown of his head. Carl's hair was short and limp, and Basil roughed the hair up after the kiss. Then he did clamp Carl's head in a headlock, but a softish headlock, and said, "You had us worried, stud."

"Glad to know it."

"You really had us worried."

"Worried's not so bad to be."

"There's worse, I reckon. I really did miss your silly ass, studly. Really did."

"That so? Missed my ass, huh? Now, what *is* your name again?"

"Yuck. Yuck. Let's get a good look-see at your boo-boo."

I handed them each a can of beer. Granny and Glenda startled up on the white blanket and scooted closer to the tree. They put fire to cigarettes. The chickens calmed down fast and went back to mumbling and pecking the dirt nearby. Red's boots began to stir some, hanging from the Mercury window.

"He has to hop," I said. "But not that much."

"Jesus," went Basil. He knelt before the bad leg. He held his hand above the crater but did not touch. "Je-sus! Oh, baby—what the fuck *was* it that got you?"

There came a noise from the battleship where Red cleared his throat. Yonder in the woods but close some crows got excited cawing the sundown news to other crows who did then caw back with more versions. A heavy glob of spit flew from the back window and landed loud. The long shadow laid down by the tiny house had fell in amongst other shadows and got lost in the crowd, now just part of the overall darkening.

Carl said, "Here's your chance, Ma—tell 'em."

When Carl said Ma, Ma meant Granny. Granny swelled, satisfied and pleased that he left the telling to her. She inflated a bit. She got bigger. She held a long cigarette and used it to point to parts of Carl's bad leg while she spoke.

She said, "This was in a bushy area. They was in bushes low down on some mountain that was numbered, and the heat they have over there is mighty mean and had got to kickin' ass on the boys purty awful. Carl had turned to this other boy—what was his name?"

"Detratto."

"That's it. Detratto. I-talian boy. So Carl turned to him and asked, 'Detratto, got any salt tablets?' Then here come a whoosh, but he just barely heard it comin'. Or maybe he never did hear it, only he decided he must have later on. He still ain't sure about hearin' the whoosh, but the heat and the bush are fact, and also there was bugs and other crap. So he turned and asked the I-talian boy the question about salt, and the answer he got was he woke up on a boat in the ocean. A boat that has got a hospital on it. A hospital just like one on land. But on a boat. What is that name you called your britches?"

"Utilities."

Glenda raised her thermos and poured a full cup. Red's face came to the window and leaned out to listen.

"I'll stick with 'britches.' His britches had got set on fire when the whoosh-bomb landed. The fire caused all this mess—here—and this mess here. He was knocked out cold so he didn't feel the fire, not then. The exploding part of the bomb tore the meat out of the leg, here, and left him this hole. See how deep it is? Touch a finger to it. They never found none of the meat—right, son?"

"I don't expect nobody looked, Ma."

"Oh, baby," went Basil. "But you can walk, can't you?"

"He walks okay," I said, "but with a hop. Doctor says he'll hop less over time."

The car door opened and out came Red slapping at his face to bring himself all the way awake. He edged behind Carl and stood there. Him joining the group changed the feel of it the way one lit match does suddenly change the feel in a hay barn.

He said, "So what happened to the dago? How'd he come out?"

"Worse."

"Uh-huh. I always knew you was the lucky dog." Red then by God squatted and grabbed on to Carl and did give him a longer hug than I thought he had it in him to give anybody, ever. His big arms added quite a bit of crush in with the hug. "What kind of dope they got you on?"

"Pills."

"What kind?"

"Three kinds."

"They give you plenty?"

"They give me plenty, but not enough."

"I hear that," Basil said.

Red rubbed Carl's hair until it laid flat.

"You need to get out of this shithole. You need to hoot'n holler. Feel like you could run around some?"

"Might could, I guess."

"No orders against it?"

"No orders I listen to."

"Well then, we could run on out to Murl's, at the junction. Or mosey on down to the Echo Club."

"Hold it, man," said Basil. "Hold it." He turned to Carl. "Both those joints feature dancin', stud. You gonna feel okay watchin' folks dancin' and shit? In your shape, I mean?"

Carl lifted his dog tags to his mouth and nipped at them with his teeth like he was checking if they were gold and they weren't so he let them fall back to his chest.

"I never did dance."

"Then throw some clothes on," Red said, laughing. "Get spruced and we'll roll."

When Carl stood I went to help him. The beer had added up and that made him need to hop more. He leaned on me heavy. At the door, he said, "That'll do, pardner."

Nightbugs had started scratching out their nightbug songs. Red and Glenda stood by the tree and he had a claw on her butt. She held her silvery cup while looking to the woods, which were black. Granny laid flat on the white blanket smoking. Basil had sat on the dirt with his toothbrush in his mouth and was trying to build Carl's pyramid of empties into a new design, something lower that swayed less and stood stronger. I sat to help him.

Glenda said, "I better nap a bit, Shug, don't you think?"

"Good idea."

"Then we'll get along on home."

"I'll be ready."

When Carl came out from the tiny house he was wearing regular clothes. Red went over and gave him a shoulder to lean on. He thumped his one claw on Carl's gut, thumping out a little peppy drum music.

"Bring your pills?"

"A few."

"All right! Ma, you best start roundin' up bail money, 'cause your boys're goin' *tonkin'* tonight!" He gave a tug on Carl and shouldered him over to the Mercury and helped him inside. "Come on, Basil, let's ride."

Basil flung an arm around me and wrestled me close. The thing he had made of Carl's tower of empties stood firm, okay, but stood only two levels tall and not much worth noticing. He yanked my head to his mouth. The toothbrush poked at my cheek when his lips moved. He whispered, *"Don't be hard to find tomorrow."*

8

WHEN I GOT CAUGHT it was in the rain. Rain had built sudden little ponds in people's yards and fresh shallow creeks to race along driveways and sidewalks. The rain fell and fell feeling warm, big loose drops falling warm, raising fingerlings of mist from paved streets. The drops busted heavy and plentiful on everything and kept up a constant racket. The sudden ponds and creeks the rain built were new problems for me to deal with, problems to leap over or slog through, to get at the next house with dope, which was a tidy average house on a street below the square.

This errand was run in the Mercury.

Basil said, "I'll bet ol' studly won't even remember her name once he comes to."

The racket from the rain had him shouting.

"If he's lucky," said Red, "her face'll be the same as her name—forgot."

The streets ran deep and the car drove feeling now and then like a rock skipping across a stream. The glass fogged right away and all I could see was a droopy gray color rolling by outside the windows. I sopped with water yet only from running to the car. We each did leak some on the car seats and make puddles on the floor.

"She's a gal whose name don't matter much, anyways. Not even to her own self."

"That's why we put them together."

"He ain't even gonna remember, ol' son."

"So? So listen, *we'll tell him* all about it! Dig? And baby, the way we run it down to him'll be way way better'n what *did* happen."

"Sure! Sure. Like, she was a Mexican beauty!"

"Man, oh man, the gal had big ol' tits with tasty pink nipples!"

"Of course, all she wore was only a pearl necklace and bikini britches and *God damn* if she didn't look a twin to Raquel fuckin' Welch."

"There you are, daddy-o. Like that. We'll feed the hero a memory along those lines. Feed him one he'll want to keep."

"Uh-huh. Instead of one that'll always make him shiver and shake if it comes to mind."

"Nope," said Red. "Nope. He don't need no more of those."

The battleship wobbled from all the water running against the tires. In the backseat I had a deviled ham sandwich. Glenda had trimmed the crust away so this was a soft easy sandwich to eat. The deviled ham was lunch and a lunch that went down fast and was not enough but was all I had. I got a slug of Basil's beer to rinse my throat.

"What was that number?" Red said. He looked at his sheet of paper, all wrinkled and spotted, then out the windshield. "Whoa, daddy-o. We just went past the fuckin' place."

I wiped a hole in the fog to look out from. The houses were okay houses and looked to have each been built by the same person in the same way.

"Which house?"

"The house right there, fat boy. The one with the li'l wood wagon full of flowers and shit in the yard. See the wagon?"

"Uh-huh."

"We'll wait up around the corner, there. Be quick."

"Ain't it still rainin' too hard?"

"No, it ain't."

"Is so! I mean—look."

"It's just fuckin' water, tub. Just water, and we ain't got forever, dig? We can't wait and wait 'til it suits your candy-ass just *per*-fect."

"And look closer this time, Shug. I do believe that last ol' boy somehow tricked you out of some mighty good dope. Just 'cause they're sick don't mean they ain't sneaky. They *can* be sneaky. So look closer."

The car door opened and Red held it wide with a booted foot while rain blew in and slapped him and me both. He turned to look me full and hard in the face while drops blew in and busted on us rat-a-tat-tat, and this look between us held a spell.

"Get."

IT seems this victim saw me coming. I came up the creek running down the drive, the water deeper than that knob-bone in the ankle, then splashed sideways to the yard, which was a mud pond my feet sank into fast. The *Grit* satchel hung off my shoulder and flopped in the wind and the rain whipped on me with no sign of quit. I guess the sick person watched the whole time. I guess he saw my feet pull from the pond, sneakers hauling tracts of mud, then watched me kick and wiggle to shed the mud while that rain whipped and whipped on me. There would then be the next steps taken and more of the same.

Instead I was in a hurricane hunting survivors from the shipwreck.

Stuff floated away in all that water. Toys of two or three lightweight types and bright colors swept away along the street. Trees had bent low to hide from the beating. Flowers were trying to fall out of that wood wagon in the yard, their frazzled heads and long necks bent over the side crying uncle.

Instead I was walking up the Mississippi River to stomp Mike Fink's ass bloody and become his best friend.

Around back the steps to the door were slick. The door was down the steps in a small square spot that seemed like a concrete sink. The door came right open and I guess the phone upstairs started dialing. Water lapped up to the heel of the door frame and tried to lap inside with me.

When I moved, my feet squeaked. There was nothing dry on me and dripping drops hit the floor sounding like applause that came during the wrong part of the song. The room was plenty gloomy and smelled of the wet. There were puffy chairs and a couch and a thing that looked to be a bar made of barrels. A bar for leaning on to drink booze. The room lay quiet but for my drips and squeaks.

I walked on tiptoes to stunt the squeaks. Across the floor three or four stairs rose to the next part of the house. Carpet had been spread on the steps. The carpet was the type that resembled shaggy mussed hair, but orange in color. When I paused standing on the carpet the applause of drops sounded faraway.

A short hall went past a small kitchen. Voices could be heard but they had that perfect sound of voices on TV. The only light came from a room ahead of me and in such a dark storm shadows thrashed all around. I went towards the voices on TV. The carpet ended of a sudden, which I did not note in time. Drops from me hit the hardwood and the man heard the applause and looked up from his chair in front of the TV.

"*Grit*, is it?" he said. He had on a plaid robe where most of the plaid was blue, and pale slippers. His hair laid close to his skull, short and fuzzy silver hair, and he wore black glasses. The TV show was a soap and he had a smoke going. "So you're the *Grit* boy."

"I'm *a Grit* boy."

"Have it your way, kid. Tell me everything about *Grit*."

"What? You never seen a *Grit*, mister?"

"I want to hear how you sell it. Your pitch. For instance, describe the journalistic merits of your publication."

There were several windows to the street but nothing to see besides the storm. Some medicine had been gathered on a stand clear on the far side of the man. Several bottles of the sort pills came in, or maybe a powder. Rain beat on the windows and shadows thrashed and the room seemed tight. Too tight to edge past him and grab the dope and edge past him again to get out and away.

"You aren't selling me, kid."

"Mister, you know *Grit*. Farmer things. Farmer jokes, stuff like that."

He wagged his head to make me think he was thinking about it. He held the cigarette raised to just beside his glasses so the smoke looked to be leaking from his ear.

"Hmm. I'd say I already know plenty of farmer jokes."

"These are fresh."

"All farmer jokes are ancient, kid."

"These are *printed* fresh—okay? Okay? I'm goin' to have to get along. I think I gotta get."

"In this downpour? There's soup on the stove—would you bring me a bowl?"

"What's wrong with you that you can't get it? Huh?"

He mashed one butt and lit another. The ashtray was made in a horseshoe shape and held plenty of mashed butts. A tall white coffee cup sat on the side table next to his cigarette pack.

"Cancer, kid. Cancer of the bone."

"Which bone?"

"Jesus, kid—all of them. It gets all of them."

"Oh."

"With crackers. Crackers are in the cupboard above the toaster."

I had to get at that dope and get it to Red. I had to get this batch to keep from being beat. I couldn't deal him another letdown. Even Basil had gotten cranky at me. This dope would have to be taken on the sly in some way I hadn't thought of yet.

"Is the soup hot?"

"I prefer it just warm. A nice big bowl, kid."

Pictures of people who must have mattered to the man stood all over a shelf along the wall. A picture from a war hung above the shelf and showed soldiers atop a hill wrestling with a flag on a pole, trying to stand the pole so it stood straight in the mud. Down the wall there hung a cloth swatch inside glass and a frame, and on the cloth words had been sewn—"We Shall Gather on the Golden Shore."

"Where would the bowls be?"

"The cupboard left of the sink. I like the yellow bowls best. Grab a bowl for yourself, kid."

"I *didn't* get much lunch."

"Have some soup and crackers."

"It was practically *nothin'* of a lunch."

"So have a *big* bowl of soup and crackers."

"Maybe I will."

"Bring mine first."

The soup was in a bright shiny pan on the stove. Just a thin streak of fat floated over the broth. I turned on the gas burner. The soup was chicken and noodles. Lots of chunks of chicken showed amidst the noodles. The fat started to blend. It seemed plenty warm in only a minute. I pulled the crackers down, scooped the man a bowl of soup and carried it back to him.

"Now I'll get mine."

"Get the door first. I just heard a car pull up."

"In this rain?"

"You might as well get the door. It's for you."

"For *me*?"

"It's the cops, kid."

"How?"

"You are exactly like your description in *The Scroll*—don't you read? I called them soon as I saw you." He wiggled sideways in the chair and a pistol butt came into view. A hefty shiny pistol. "I thought I might have to shoot you, and I didn't really want to. I wouldn't say you *need* shooting—but you are in a mess of trouble."

I tried to flee by running out the way I snuck in. My feet thundered through the house and I splashed up the concrete steps and a heavy cop in a rain slicker stood there holding a billy club.

He said, "You make me chase you in all this mud and shit and I'll smack you silly. You hear me?"

I just about did run anyhow, but stopped instead.

"Call my mom."

"Don't worry, boy, your mom'll get called." He grabbed me by the wrist and yanked me down the creek in the drive to the cop car. Another cop stood there and the one that had me said, "He didn't run, at least."

"He didn't, huh?" This other cop was the one named Herren, but this time he was wet and not so kindly-seeming. The drops caught on his mustache and made it sag further so his mouth moved out of sight. "Ah, I know who this dumpling is, anyhow. Red Akins's boy, ain't you? Where *is* that rotten bum Red?"

"Couldn't say."

"You never have made no trouble before on your

own, have you?"

"Huh-uh."

"So where's Red?"

I looked around at the rain that gushed over us all, and the sudden ponds and creeks, the acres of mud.

"Playin' golf, I reckon."

"Ain't he cute?"

"He's real cute."

"See if he's cute in cuffs."

The victim in blue plaid had come out on his front porch and stood where the roof covered him. He waved his cigarette at me. He shouted through the storm, "Thanks for the soup, kid!"

Herren said, "Cuff the cute dumpling and throw him in the back."

I was spun around rough, my arms pulled behind me, the cuffs put on, and as they snapped shut, making that click that means it's no use to fight, I knew I had been caught, and caught good, and at that exact second I felt my bones wilt and the meat and muscles of me go limp and sag.

"Not here," I said. "Red's not here."

9

THEY ASKED ME QUESTIONS they knew I could not answer. Two of them did sit with me, one beside me on both sides. We sat that way in the front main room of the station. Windows in there reached from the floor to the roof and the roof was up a ways, so rain had a long spread of glass to break across and pour down. We sat along the wall on a wood bench that had been picked at and gouged by many many people passing time in rocky moods.

"Does Red sell this stuff off to other assholes, too, or do him and Basil Powney hog it all for their own dumbshit sort of fun?"

"I just wonder, how many of them pills is it a wild feller like you might swoller at one time?"

"Where do they go to loaf these days?"

All I ever did answer to either of them was, "Just get my mom."

She came into the station wet. She'd had to walk. Her raven hair was plastered by rain to her neck and face, and she was carrying an umbrella that had been ripped to start with and in the storm had become just a polished stick with some tatters on one end. Her feet were soaked and the weather had made a mess of makeup on her cheeks.

She came straight to the bench where they had left me, shaking herself as she came, then slid close beside me.

"You didn't say anything, did you?"

"Nope."

"You know better than to say anything, right?"

"I didn't tell 'em nothin'."

"Uh-huh," she said. She pulled up her shirt showing her belly and wiped her face plain. "You've got to stand tough, sweet mister."

"I didn't tell 'em nothin'."

"Uh-huh," she said. "I knew you wouldn't. Need a smoke?"

"I guess."

She tapped one loose for herself also, and found a dry match and lit us up. She puffed and I puffed beside her until a small shared cloud was born over our heads and started to grow. The rain kept flying against the tall windows, making splat-splat sounds.

"Aw, I guess I probably better go talk to the law about you and get it over with."

"Yeah, probably better."

She left the umbrella stick laying on the bench beside me. I sat next to the stick and smoked alone. I thought being hunched over smoking a cigarette might make me look to be seriously thinking some useful thought about my situation. I tried several times to truly puff up some useful thought but none did rise clear to me. I dropped the butt into the puddle at my feet.

THE rain began to lay down and quiet. The sidewalks had been flooded kind of clean. The rush of storm water raised the loose trash from the sidewalk and carried it whatever distance, and when the water drained the litter came to rest in the street in a whole new layout of trash. Worms had gushed up from the dirt alongside the curb and plenty fled from the soaked dirt onto the paved walk and laid there beached and gasping.

Glenda and me walked away from the station in this quieter mood of rain. We walked together in the open like no rain fell at all. Already both soaked, there was no point trying to avoid the drops.

She said, "I should've known whatever he had you out doin' would surely be one wrong goddamn thing or other."

Every minute or two her hands raised to her head and raked all her fingers through her hair, raking it back from her face into a slick raven pile. Rain dripped from her long eyelashes. The blue of her eyes showed great against those long damp lashes.

I said, "Wrong as hell."

"Why didn't you tell me?"

"I told you, 'Men stuff.'"

"That's *not* tellin' me, Shug."

"You knew what it meant."

"I certainly did not."

"Maybe not exactly. But, more or less, you knew."

A pickup truck splashed beside us with a sopping old hound dog standing in the bed. The dog and me caught each other's eyes and the hound looked like he reckoned that at some other time him and me could be friends and yell at squirrels together. Even when the truck splashed off a good ways down the road he looked back at me.

"You can't ever let Red even *wonder* if you might rat on him, sweet mister. *Not ever.*"

"I don't rat."

"Please, please, listen—don't let it flit across his brain that you might even *think* of rattin' on him."

Robins had spotted the gasping worms on the sidewalks, and dived onto them to feast. Birds suddenly were whirling around in the air, diving and shoving each other out of the way on the paved walk, choking down lengths of big fat worms.

"I didn't tell 'em nothin'."

"Shug, these ex-cons, they really got a bad opinion on anybody that talks."

"I know *that*."

"Rats come in for awful rough treatment from them."

A couple of robins did get so lost in gorging on beached worms that they sat there feasting yet when I walked up, so I took the worms' side and kicked at them, and when they popped into the air flapping I swung, too, but did not land with either the kicks or the punches.

"I ain't got no fuckin' rat in me, Glenda. So drop it."

"I know you don't," she said. "I know. Just, we can't ever let Red wonder if maybe you *do*."

"God, I hate him."

A car slowed in the street beside us. It was that Thunderbird, green, from the legendary era. The driver leaned to the passenger door and opened it. The car interior was a beautiful bright perfect white. The man called to us, "Lord Almighty, folks, come in from the rain. You'll catch your deaths walkin' out there."

* * *

THE Thunderbird had the feel of laying in a fine soft bed with whitewall tires that somebody was driving smooth and sure. This car had special qualities I wouldn't have known about to ask for. Somehow the Thunderbird seemed to instantly comb the bumps from the road ahead to keep the ride always gentle. It was a fabulous make of car. I never had been so high in the world.

Glenda said, "I am so sorry. I truly am."

"About what?"

"About us bein' so drippin' wet in your car. Wet all over your seats."

"Don't worry about the seats," he said. "People come first."

He had more size than I recalled. His hands on the wheel were big-knuckled and heavy and his wrists were stout and his shoulders burly. He showed many signs of being strong but not very young. His hairs were gray and had dwindled from his head a good deal. His face looked similar to lots of other faces in a crowd, but with deep creases from laughing and dark dark eyes. He dressed in the upright style, like a fella who always had managed to find a job.

I leaned in from the backseat and asked, "Now, who is it you said you are again?"

"Jimmy Vin Pearce."

Glenda turned to me and said, "Got that now? It's rude to not remember twice."

He said, "And you're Shuggie, while the lady here is Glenda. Which surely is a pretty name."

"You think? I never have been all the way sold on it."

"It's a real pretty name."

"Hmm."

"A name that sounds like a song, even."

The windshield wipers just whispered while wiping the rain from the glass. The drops had shrunk to the size of freckles and fewer fell. Kids had come outside to the gutters in yellow raincoats and set about floating stuff in the rapids along the curb, racing to the drains.

"I don't know the streets here too well," he said. "You'll have to point the way for me."

"Where are you from?" she asked.

"You mean lately? Or to start with?"

"Whichever."

"Originally from Phenix City. That's not Phoenix, Arizona. It's Phenix City, Alabama. I came around here to cook at the Echo Club."

"Since when are you the cook at the Echo Club?"

"A few months now. I had been at a hotel in St. Louis, but that went sour 'cause I got my own ideas about paprika, when it's right and when it's just plain wrong, and a customer there says to me if I'd come down to West Table I could cook at the Echo Club. So, what the hey, here I am."

"Cook always seems a funny job for a man to me."

"There's nothing funny about it."

"Is that what you always have been? A cook?"

"For twenty years or a little more. I've cooked all over. Seen lots of places. *Plenty* of cooks are men. I got started over in Kentucky. Covington, Kentucky, was Las Vegas before Vegas amounted to diddly, you know. It used to be real real lively. I cooked at the Lookout House there."

Glenda squealed and clapped her hands.

"Sleepout Louie's?" she said.

"Ho-ho," he went, and looked at her sharp, "you know *Covington*?"

"Uh-huh." Her eyes lit up and her posture came alive. She twisted on the white seat until she'd twisted facing him flush. "When I was a kid girl I waited tables at the Beverly Club."

"Holy cow, the casino? Good money for those days, I'll bet."

"Great dough. Good dough for these days, even."

"The Beverly Club—didn't Baron Ambers run that joint?"

"Sure did," she said. "The Baron was a great man."

"He was nobody to mess with. I used to see him around, in different spots. He was part of the Cleveland bunch."

"He sure was."

"That was the right bunch to be with in that town."

"Mostly. Mostly that was so. You need to turn this way."

About here they each lit cigarettes and ran off into the past and talked different memories at each other. I listened some, but not too close. Somebody they'd both heard of was dead, and so was somebody else, and there were things said about big spenders and girls who'd hooked live ones and how things change.

I kept silent hoping people I knew would see me riding in such a car.

At a stop sign the man said, "Is he named after the Baron for a reason? Or just 'cause he's lucky?" He had a little smile on when he turned to look at me. His little smile flattened. "Ah."

A street later he said, "He had his trouble in—what?—what year?"

"'Fifty-five."

"Oh, yeah. I was on my way out by then."

"The whole town was on its way out by then."

"Yes, ma'am. The good days were done."

"You follow everybody else to Vegas?"

"No. No. I tried Cuba for a month, but I'm not that great with seafood. Besides, gamblin's more fun when it's illegal. At least to me. When it's legal it gets to be about like goin' to a church that's gotten just a *little teensy-bit* mixed up about a couple of things, but is *still* a church."

"I came home," Glenda said. "Here. Back to this."

"Which way now?"

"Stop anywhere, I guess. We live up in that house in the cemetery. You'll sink in the drive if you pull in."

I got out and stood there touching the car.

She had one foot in the car and one foot in the mud.

"Thank you so much, Jimmy Vin."

"No problem, ma'am."

He gave her a piece of white paper.

"If you ever need a free steak dinner, folks, I'll do you up proud at the Echo Club. Call me at that number there, anytime. Kitchen closes at nine, so try to come before."

"Okay," she said, "we might do it."

He waved so long and drove on down the road. The wonder of that T-bird made the wet road sit up straight and wipe its face and wink.

"Goodness, but there goes one nice, nice man," she said. "Don't you think? Notice his watch?"

I said, "He was nice enough. But Glenda—that man shouldn't *ever ever* show his face around here again."

She stamped her feet in the mud several times and splashed brown drops. For a minute she dismissed that I was there. She stared towards the house. She stared towards the house and stomped several splatters of mud that only dirtied her own legs.

She said, "He is so goddamn hateful."

10

THE SUN CAME AROUND, the grass grew fast, I had work to do. The sun shined steady for days and with all the storm water poured on it the grass seemed practically to bubble up foamy like the head on a root beer. The color of this foamy head, though, was a healthy summer green.

Glenda did help, or did try to help in the ways she thought helped. She picked up twigs and tossed them into a pile. She somewhat snipped the thin edges of grass the mower missed, scooting about on her knees in the clean sunlight, humming and snipping. She found three lost coins worth eleven cents. Now and then she fetched drinks from the house.

At times she went adrift on her thoughts in the tractor's path and had to be hollered at to move.

"Glenda, I can do this by myself."

"No, no, hon—I want to help."

"But I have my own certain order I get this done."

"Well, I could use the exercise. I want to work off this li'l pooch on my tummy. See this pooch?"

"Your tummy don't pooch."

"Not as much since I've been helping you, hon. The work in this heat trims that pooch away. All that crouching and standing. Bending. I do want to start lookin' my best again."

The first of the sick people I robbed came to be buried on one of those fine bright days. The teenager who had skin that looked fogged and a way bald head. He was buried in a plot in the olden part, in a big family plot where the dates went back a century. I'd spaded crabgrass from that section plenty of times. The stone they put over him was a shiny sort of brown, with a curly scrolled part at the top. The numbers hammered into his stone showed him to be almost nineteen. The crowd spread from the bald teenager's grave in a packed circle that went partway up the hill and into the shade thrown by a line of pine trees. Funeral crowds always did smell like the perfumes old ladies favor, the smells of fancy flowers, which were then joined by the smells from the many bunches of typical flowers folks held in their hands until time to lay the bunches atop the heap of fresh-turned dirt. As the flowers were laid down, somebody sang something in a churchy mood I did not care to hear.

"I wish they'd shut up that singin'."

"It's gospel, Shug." Glenda tapped loose cigarettes for us both and lit the lighter. The breeze made the flame bend, stand, bend, stand. "Spiritual."

"I wish they'd shut up."

"Oh, hon—can't you imagine how they must feel? Burying a boy?"

I blew out a gray cloud that didn't last much past my nose.

"Glenda, that boy was one of the sick folks I robbed dope from."

She flashed me a stunned look, cigarette at her mouth, then her face fell in on itself, sort of, and she made a choked noise louder than the gospel from where we stood, and pitched her smoke to the ground. She moved off towards the house in a hangdog posture, hands over her ears, cuss words and oaths spitting piecemeal from her lips.

The screen door whacked shut.

There was another song.

11

RED STAYED GONE A GOOD LONG WHILE, until the afternoon he drove to the house in a two-tone pickup truck, yellow and cream, drove clear to the back stoop, and said, "I believe I'll take the boy fishin'."

He spoke from inside the truck to where we sat on the concrete stoop. We'd squatted where the shade fell. He dangled one arm from the window and with the other arm raised a fist his chin rested on. He wore a store-bought sleeveless white T-shirt with a V-notched neck. His little bump of hair was combed good and oily. His eyes had that blur.

"No, huh uh," said Glenda. "I reckon he doesn't care to go fishing."

"I've come to take the boy fishin'."

"He doesn't fish. He doesn't care to *eat* fish."

"He don't gotta eat 'em, you witch."

Red gave me that steady steady look of his that left me feeling already the worms underground spiraling into my eyeballs and brain and the soft meat of me. That look he had that warned of swift death which lasts so long.

"Red," she said, "*please*. Please, Red."

"What the fuck's the deal? I'm his daddy, ain't I? Ain't a daddy s'posed to teach his boy how to fish and shit? Ain't he? Ain't he s'posed to? And since I'm *daddy* to *Morris* there, I reckon it falls to me to teach him. Don't it? You see it different?"

"This is baloney," she said. "I've never known you to ever bother with fish, neither—why now?"

"Would you quit, huh? Quit tryin' to come between a *daddy* and his *boy*."

I could only wonder where the truck came from. It had a gruff rumbling engine, four on the floor, and a thin spread of smelly straw lay in the bed around a plywood dog-box that did not contain a dog. A white ice chest sat on the straw.

"It's easier if I just go."

"WHY'RE we pickin' *her* up?"

"She's comin' along."

"What do we want her for?"

"She's got the rods, dig?"

Full summer heat was in play that day. Folks moved slower. Dogs crawled under porches and would not fetch. People got cranky about other people blocking the fan wind. Tar patches on the road bubbled up like black pancakes almost ready to flip. Anything around that did not smell too good normally smelled awful.

"When's your juvie court?"

"I don't know. Not so far off, though."

Patty did not wave when we pulled in. She dropped a cigarette and stepped on it, then she spun about and picked up a brown sack. She had her hair down and it was down nearly to her butt. Her clothes were jeans and an orange shirt with green leaves from a beach-type tree on it and sneakers that couldn't be hurt any worse.

Red went over and kissed at her. His kiss only hit her

cheek because she turned her mouth away.

"Go on and pout, princess. Comin' or not?"

"You're late."

"Now why in hell do you bother tellin' me that?"

I got out to let her in. He tossed an armload of stuff that clattered into the truck bed. The sack she carried smelled like food. She sat in the middle of the cab, her legs apart around the shifter on the floor. By the time we reached the city limits her left hand had creeped up to Red's neck and her fingers went to tickling around his little ducktail of hair.

Some miles into the drive she said, "I've never been introduced to you, young man."

"You don't gotta be."

Red said, "You want a bloody nose, tub? You tell her howdy, and tell her your name."

The woods had tightened around the road. The woods would not let you see anything much that wasn't right next to the road, and only a little ways ahead and a little ways back.

"Howdy. Shuggie."

"Okay. That's okay, Red. He said it. Just call me Patty."

The road was gray but seemed polished by the sun and weaved us along between thick broody woods and up the long hills and along the crestline where way way below lay a river cut between rock bluffs. The river caught the sunlight and reflected it in a dull shade of golden. Then the woods closed in again like a tunnel until we rolled downhill and came to a black skeleton bridge with a floor of wide pale lumber planks that jittered as we drove across. A sign read "Twin Forks River."

She said, "I don't guess I've seen this river in three years, or more."

"Has it changed any?"

"Why, no. No."

"Then you didn't miss nothin'."

After the bridge the road became a dirt road. The woods in this stretch had been thinned and the grass mowed. There were a few picnic tables, a water pump, and an outhouse. Red spit at this civilized spot and drove beyond it along a skinny road with deep ruts. This path was one vehicle wide and tall weeds leaned into it to scratch at the truck when we went by. Finally the path opened onto a flat riverbank of small rocks on this side facing high watchful rock bluffs across the water.

A large blackish bird with a pale neck the length of three or four necks flapped up real gawky from the water's edge and winged away down the river gulch.

Red parked there, on the rocks, facing the bluffs.

"Get in the glove box, babe, and hunt me up a yellowjacket."

"Just one?"

"For now."

THE river flowing past at my feet sounded like nice women close by whispering friendly together and made me feel welcome. I tossed broken limbs into the water and watched them flow happy downstream and disappear. The water moved along pretty brisk, with waves like the waves in cake frosting, and the rocks I threw did not skip across too great. The smell was similar to how well-water smells, only with a mess of weeds and fish adding their flavors to the scent.

The fishing gear was jumbled and hard to ready. Red and Patty hunkered on the rocks, fussing with the tangle, smokes stuck to their lips.

"This stuff was all Dave's," she said. "He didn't take it when he left."

"I believe I'm gonna need a beer to figure out the mess ol' *Dave* made of this shit."

"Comin' up."

Fish heads laid scattered on the small rocks. Their eyes had been picked clean and their skin swallowed too. The sun had baked the skull parts to a dainty creepy whiteness. They felt very light and did not fly far when pitched.

She said, "Red, honey, I don't believe you use bobbers on a river."

"I dig bobbers."

"But on a river, you know, they're bobbin' all the time. From the current. If they bob all the time, well, then the bobbin' don't tell you a thing."

"Bobbers and worms is about all I know about this shit. *Fishin'*. I never had nobody to show me. I pulled my first bit at fourteen. They didn't teach fishin' there. Anyhow, fuckin' fish, who cares?"

She bent, rubbed his neck, and said, "I like 'em pan-fried. With hash browns."

"You know what I like? I like yellowjackets—get me another."

* * *

THE next thing was bait.

Red said, "Give me your knife, boy. We'll just rustle us some worms right quick."

I brought my knife out and flicked the blade open. I held it firm. This knife used to be his, years back. The blade was thin and shined. I held it about a foot from his belly and he grinned at me, a slow shallow grin, then took the knife from my hand.

"Nice ol' blade," he said. "Course the deal with blades is, you gotta have the balls to use 'em."

Back from the river, where the beach of small rocks ended, the woods began again. A short ridge of dirt lay like a rumple between the rock beach and the treeline. The glinting sunlight had those rocks looking valuable. The ridge of dirt was a washed-down brown color. The ridge was soft and the dirt lip would crumble away if you stood there.

Red kneeled by the ridge and started to stab at it. He sank the blade all the way. This part of fishing he enjoyed. He twisted the blade, went in and out, scaling dirt from the ridge, stabbing over and over. He sank the blade and pulled sideways like he was gutting a nightwatchman but expected buckets of worms to tumble out instead of guts.

There were no worms.

I could see my blade had got twisted.

No worms would live on the edge of a crumbling ridge.

"Screw this noise," Red said. He tossed the knife

onto the rocks for me to fetch. "Piss on it—too much like work for me."

Patty said, "They live under things. Back a ways, in the good dirt."

"You want to go dig 'em?" Red went to the brown sack of picnic food. He dropped a claw in and felt around the sack. "What's to eat in here?"

"Burgers. Just homemade burgers."

When his claw rose from the bag it held a pinch of burger. The burger pinch was near the size of an unshelled walnut. He grabbed a fishing line and tracked along it to the fish hook, then stuck the hook into the entire pinch of burger.

Patty went, "I don't care to ever meet the fish that would eat *that*."

"If you're fixin' to laugh at me you best make damn sure I don't hear."

Neither of the reels on the rods worked. Red carried the hook to where the bobber clung to the line. He held the hook and bobber together, stepped to the river's edge, then pitched the bobber and the burger out on the stream and they carried the line between them. The stuff landed near the middle of the water. The bobber seemed to rattle away on the fast flow. The flow soon swung the bobber in towards the riverbank only maybe twenty feet from where Red and me stood.

He said, "They brung me in and kept me eight hours, boy. They'd love to hang that rap on me. They'd love that." We watched the bobber stray to the very very shallow water a yard or so from the rock beach and it bobbed gentler there, but was pointless. "Now Shug,

you wouldn't never, you know, snitch on your ol' da . . .
Red. You wouldn't snitch on ol' Red, would you?"

"I didn't."

"I mean ever."

"Don't I know better?"

"You should."

THE bobber stayed where it first landed, butting slow
and easy against the rocks in the shallows. We ate and
drank and the bobber never went any farther. She
talked about people she did not like who worked at the
hospital and he said, Yeah. Oh, yeah? The fuckers. The
burgers were okay, with cheese. I had a beer from the
ice chest, a kind with a fox face on the can, and they
each did drink a few to my one. They soon began to
hug and lick back and forth.

Red said, "Hey, tub, why don't you get your ass in
the water some? Probably feels good, I bet."

The river was not so wide but I could not see bottom
all the way across. In the deep parts the water rippled
less. The water seemed clear but in a hurry.

"I can't swim."

"You can't? You can't swim? Not a lick?"

"I can't even float."

He leaned sideways as if in thought, which maybe
he was. He then nodded his head.

"So don't go out too far—it can't be very deep."

"Plus I just ate."

"I'll keep a eye on you."

"Don't they say if you just ate . . ."

"Aw, go on and get in the river, fat boy. Jesus. Show

some fuckin' sand." She started to say something but he hit her with a swift look that snapped her mouth shut fast. "Go on! Go on, would you?"

The rock bluffs had laid down shadow that colored the far part of the river darker. A few times a fish or something went past rooting for eats along the rock bottom. The water had that sound of women who wouldn't hurt me. That sound of voices in talk that I could join. I shuffled towards the voices, up to my knees, and a little farther, and more.

Springs from inside the earth caused this river. It was made of old old water and ran cold. The cold at first seemed too much, but soon it was not so bad, later great. I sat on the rocky bottom cross-legged where the water leveled just under my chin.

When I looked back to the picnic, him and her were not there. They stood beside the truck clutched together nasty. A door hung open. She backed inside the door and all the while he was getting at her. He hefted her onto the seat and she settled on her back. The door blocked most of the nasty clutching from me. But her feet dangled below the open door and her jeans soon puddled around her old sneakers. One foot then kicked free and the jeans slid to the rocks. His britches fell and wadded around his boots. His head dipped below the door frame and he went up on his toes and lunged out of sight.

The river had become a place of comfort to me. My body got tuned to the temperature and the water took only a short while to show the very very nice side of such coolness in summer. Some waves jumped high, past the chin to the mouth, and I tasted the river and it tasted about right.

Once I sat still, gang after gang of little fish stopped by to nibble, to pucker and nibble, on the vast white belly-skin I offered. They lined around my tummy. They pecked under my arms. They gathered like a pack to pucker and nibble at the fat rolls on my chest. I had the right flavor for them. The fish were small narrow things, some creamy with dark stripey parts, others pure yellow, and all moved fast. The fish made me feel like a special treat, like if I did float and laid myself in the current and drifted they'd come with, come along, a pack of fish traveling in the shadow beneath me as I floated and floated away.

"Hey, pick up your shit," he said. "We're goin'."

She did not look at me straight. He wouldn't wait for me to dry. Bent cans laid around. One burger had been chewed on but not finished and had fallen apart on the rocks. She wadded the brown sack. He put the ice chest in the truck.

"Just forget ol' *Dave's* junk," he said. "Shit didn't work even a little."

We sat in the truck the same as before, her in the middle. He drove like his hands were sticky, slow to pull loose and move from steering wheel to gearshift, and his eyes had a bright sincere blur. It seemed she fell to sleep or close to sleep, her head drooping his way. The sun dropped behind the bluffs. We went down the skinny lane and the weeds scratched at the truck. When we came to the black skeleton bridge over the river he slowed the truck to a crawl, then leaned and looked my way. The blur of his eyes called for my total attention.

He said, "Now, Basil—there's a fella with *no* fuckin' responsibilities. Huh-uh. Huh-uh. There ain't nobody at all countin' on *him*. No, sir. Nobody."

The bridge jittered plenty loud as we crossed.

12

KIDS HAD HELD A PARTY in the bone orchard near the black angel and busted beer bottles against the tombstones and littered. Most likely it was high school kids. Mr. Goynes found their mess first and fell by at noon to rag on Glenda and me for not hearing the kids in the night and chasing them away. That is what we're here for he said four or five times. That is why we get to live in this house. That is what he must be able to trust us to do.

The black angel was a special grave marker over across the way, inside a circle of pines, and probably only a champion hound dog or a old lady with sleep troubles could have heard the party sounds from there to our house. The black angel stood ten feet tall and stood over a mass grave of mostly teenagers who'd gone to a dancehall to dance years and years and years ago when dynamite or gas or who knows what exploded the dancehall and the teenagers became charcoal chunks nobody could recognize as any particular person. Twenty-eight of the dancers did lay beneath the black angel and there always were live kids who hoped maybe the black angel had taken on spooky powers from standing over such a large party of dead young. The kids sat candles at the angel's feet. They sang things to her. They put lipstick on her lips. Drips of wax lined her cheeks like frozen tears. Cigarette stubs and chip bags and the like littered the plot. The beer bottles had been busted so beer would splash on the big grave and sink for those many thirsty dead dancers.

After Mr. Goynes left, me and Glenda fetched a garbage can. The can was the burly gray metal kind, and she took one handle and me the other. We half dragged the can way over to the mess around the black angel.

"So happy fuckin' birthday," I said, "to you."

"This will not spoil it, Shug."

The weather had gotten into a perfect mood. The heat felt just right in a T-shirt. The sky stretched pure blue from end to end. The grass smelled good.

"This is sure 'nough a mess," she said. Candles had melted into hard puddles on the stone base under the angel's feet. Glass pieces had flown about for some distance and hid in the grass. "If we get it picked up fast we could still make ourselves that cake."

"The cake's up to you, Glenda—how old are you?"

"I was still a child when you were born."

I flicked my blade open to scrape candle wax off the angel. She started to collect trash and drop it in the can.

"Are you twenty-nine?"

"That's a nice age. But huh-uh."

"Are you thirty?"

"My age isn't for the public to know, hon."

"Thirty-one?"

"Stop—you're one guess from makin' me lie to you, and I'd rather not."

"Is that the truth?"

She had both hands cupped around a load of glass

bits which she let fall into the can.

"You smarty-pants, hush."

We got busy finding the mess and dumping it in the can. I could not reach the angel's face so the frozen tears and lipstick would have to be cleaned away by time. Glenda was up and down, up and down, stretching her legs to spring about, working herself like gym class, dropping trash into the can.

"Look," she said. I did look and she stood sideways to me, presenting a view of herself all pulled in and scenic. "No more pooch. See?"

"Uh-huh." I was parched of a sudden. Thirsty for cola or water or whatever, and cotton-mouthed. "If you did pooch it'd sure 'nough show in *them* shorts. And it don't."

"Thank you, sweet mister."

I guess the mess took most of an hour to clean. We kept busy bending and scraping and kneeling and standing. She slid looks my way pretty often and seemed to be wondering something but did not say much. Dragging the can back to the house was hard and we paused for breath a few times, and during one of the pauses she asked, "Shug, have you, you know—don't be embarrassed—but do you have hair comin' in yet?"

"Huh?"

"Do you have hair on your privates yet?"

"For chrissake, Glenda!"

"I guess you do, don't you?"

"I'm thir-*teen*! That ain't a baby, you know."

"No, no, of course it's not."

"I got hair, too. I got hair the same as any man does."

She grinned and pouted her lips out. She rubbed my head. She laughed a gentle laugh.

"But you're not the same as any man, Shug. You're not. You're my sweet mister, see, and that's special."

"Only to you," I said. "Far as I can tell."

"And don't you think that's just about perfect, hon? Don't you?"

I could not look at her and answered by moving. I moved to the gray trashcan and grabbed it in a hug, my arms around to both handles, and lifted it from the ground and hefted it alone towards the shed, straining and groaning, kicking and grunting, and she did not say another thing but I did see she smiled.

THE cake she most went for had icing that went on pink, with cherry halves stuck in it. She cooked the cake parts. She mixed the icing in my bowl and dripped in cherry juice that caused the pinkness. She spread the icing on the cake stack. I plunked the red red cherries into the pink in a design I did not recognize myself until halfway round the cake.

"I need more sweet cherries."

"You used the whole bottle. That's plenty. What is it you're tryin' to make?"

"Like domino numbers on the side, a big star on top."

"You're sort of close, hon."

"If I had more cherries . . ."

"It's perfect now."

"It's *not* perfect."

"It's done, I mean."

She gave me the icing bowl so I could lick the smears clean. I used a finger and made a quick job of it. She smoked staring out the screen door. Her eyes aimed up so I guess it was the sky that had caught her attention. When she blew out, a sound was let loose with the smoke, a not-so-happy sigh, I guess, but short of a moan.

I said, "What would you dream for if you could get it?"

"Too many things."

"Like what?"

"Oh, Shug, I don't know. Anyhow, most of what we call dreams are really *wants*. A want's real different from a dream. I'm not sure *which* is most likely to have an answer show up."

I stood by her looking out the screen door and she held her cigarette to my lips for one puff. I let the smoke slip from my mouth in thin trickles.

"Okay, then—what do you *want*?"

"What I truly want I wouldn't say out loud."

"Say it silent, then."

"Already did."

She walked to the john and I heard the cigarette hiss when it hit the tiny pond. She came straight back to the kitchen. She laid her arms around me completely, snuggled me close in a warm standing hug. She kissed light kisses at my hair. Her hands cradled my neck.

"No need to wait," she said. "Let's eat cake."

* * *

HE showed up with silk. He showed up with other swag, also, but the silk was what mattered. He arrived in the battleship with Basil, who helped him tote the swag inside. They arranged a short column of boxes that held toasters, and a pile of men's suit coats they then flanked with two bulging shopping bags. Basil had received a new cut on his chin that made a sloppy scab that did not seem dry. Red moved around like his ribs hurt, sort of hunched and slow when turning. Once the swag was in the kitchen they opened beer bottles from the fridge and looked at their take laid out on the floor. Red soon squatted slow and easy beside a shopping bag. He said, "Happy birthday, girl. Got somethin' for you."

"No thanks."

"Wait 'til you see it." He sent a claw into a black bag that had a store name printed in white on the side, then pulled up a yellow girl's shirt. "This 'un here'd be *my* pick."

"Umm, is . . . is that *silk*?"

"You bet," went Basil. "We didn't go out huntin' silk, you know, but when we run across it, Red there, Red thought of *you*. So we glommed some."

She put one hand down on a hip while the other hand was held up alongside a cheek. She seemed to go wandering in her head for a bit. The color in her face shifted. She hummed one small part of a song two or three times, then said, "*Real* silk? *All* silk? Or some part-silk baloney?"

Red said, "It's as much silk as silk gets. Total pure Oriental silk from somewhere over there. Plus, I always dig this color on you."

"You do?"

"It makes your eyes shine better'n most jewelry does."

Her hands slid up and down and all across that silk. She stroked the Oriental shirt like it might purr or grant three wishes. She raised the silk and nuzzled it with her nose.

"Good Lord, but this stuff feels fine. I always have craved silk. I guess you know that. Silk, silk *means* something."

"Go slip it on, girl. Give us a good peek at you dressed in fresh yaller silk. Go on. It's yours now, dig?"

"I guess I will."

Glenda took her birthday gift and left the kitchen for the bedroom and shut the door.

"She's tickled," Basil said. "Good thing you remembered."

"I don't know why I did."

"Nice you did."

Basil bent over the sink and splashed his face and gave his teeth a few strokes with his brush. Red looked at me and looked like I had suddenly improved in his eyes or he had suddenly reached just the right degree of stoned. His expression surely did confuse me. Glenda's smokes sat on the table and I pulled one and lit it as his claws came down on my shoulders and tightened.

"So tell me, boy, what's that witch got up to lately?"

"Only what she oughta be up to."

"Which would be what?"

"House stuff. Cemetery stuff."

His claws clenched tighter on me.

"You know, boy, we don't get on so well, her and me, but I just plain *love* that witch."

I looked down once he said that and his claws quickly fell away from me and I moved to the screen door. Three squirrels chased each other in circles on the roof of the shed. The trees in the yard rustled in an easygoing breeze and the breeze rolled on through the screen and fanned my face. The back window of the Mercury on the passenger side had been busted out. There was another armload of silk things on the backseat, silk things intended, I do imagine, for somebody else.

Basil said, "Where'd you get the cig, Shug?"

"Glenda's pack. On the table."

"Think she'd mind if I mooched one?"

Red said, "You don't even gotta ask that."

Both of them took her cigarettes and raised their beer bottles and leaned against the sink.

Glenda returned dressed different from top to bottom. She'd put on black slacks that clung on her snug, clung mighty snug, and shoes with high heels and the yellow silk shirt. Her hair had been brushed beautiful. The silk laid on her great, wonderful, and she posed, sort of, to show us.

Red went, "My, my."

"You like?" she asked. I'd say she looked to where I stood. "It suits me?"

"Yup," I said. "Yup."

"My, my." He got to her and put her in a big hug. "You're lookin' hot, girl." The hug kept her stuck in his arms, then his claws began to roam and he felt of her in different places, then grabbed her butt with both claws and lifted. "Happy birthday."

"Don't."

"Don't *what*?"

"*Paw me* in front of everybody."

"Then they better get, and get *now*, 'cause I'm fixin' to unwrap this package and enjoy."

She just went poof, deflated in his arms, fell limp in his hug.

Basil touched a hand to my neck and steered me towards the door.

"Come on, kid, what say we stags go out back of the shed and talk about baseball matters?"

All the windows in the house were open to the screens. Sounds carried to the yard. For a brief moment me and Basil stood beside the battleship, hearing things, staring at our toes, rubbing our faces, then he slapped the car.

"Shit, Shug, I can't hang around and listen to Red tom-cat in there. I'm gonna have to get gone, and this minute, too. You're on your own, ol' son."

I could not stand there too long alone.

I walked clean to the black angel.

"BUD'S Smoke Stak," Red said. The three of us sat at the kitchen table, those two with cigarettes burning. "Remember Bud's Smoke Stak?"

"Down at the lake," she said. "What about it?"

"Let's eat there. I got a nice payday in my pocket, girl. A nice choker of green. So let's us cruise over to the lake and chow down on a big ol' pile of ribs."

"That's a pretty fair drive, Red."

"So?"

"It's a ways to go. It's already late for supper."

"Ain't tonight special? I'd say it is. Don't you? Ain't it? Huh?"

He put us in the truck with her in the middle.

She said, "I hate sittin' like this."

"Like what?"

"You know—my legs split around the shifter."

"You'll come to like it okay, I bet."

The sun was low and pointed in our eyes for some miles. Outside of town he turned onto roads that were new to me. I did not recognize anyplace. The truck muttered deep mutters and carried us past ponds and hog pens and barking dogs and over rock ridges and trim quiet creeks and into darkening woods. He took a gravel road that went sideways from the paved road and pushed on along it at a fast speed.

Here and there he tried to talk as if we all were fond of each other.

"So now, boy, what is it you're gonna tell to the juvie judge?"

"'Just goofin' around, Your Honor. Sorry.'"

"And who's your crime partners?"

"'Nobody. Solo lobo, Your Honor.'"

The gravel road ran into a concrete road and Red turned right onto the pavement. This road had once been the main highway to somewhere and now was nothing much except the slow back way to still get there. It was the olden style of slab highway. The concrete was poured in chalk-white slabs and the slabs were joined together but they never fit together perfect. This meant tires went thump at the seams, thump at each new slab, thump 'cause hardly any slabs laid together smooth. Some of the seams had split to where things grew up between the slabs.

"Red," she said, "we're awful hungry."

"You'll get fed."

"We were hungry when we started."

"Just think about Bud's ribs and cold beer."

"But . . . I don't recall this bein' the way to the lake."

"I gotta see a fella first."

"Aw, no. No."

"Don't start whinin' 'til you been hurt."

At a crossroads there stood a filling station that had been put there when this road was the main route. There was a faded horse with wings on the sign. The sign showed splashes of rust. The wood of the building had aged and lost its paint. The place stood cocked some to the side and the roof had a swayback. Out front there were two whitish gas pumps and an old man sitting on a bench by the door.

The old man waved and we each waved back.

"There it is," Red said. He said that about a dirt road, more of a cow path, just beyond the filling station. "This is where we turn."

THE road was a skinny streak of dirt that carried us past a few farmhouses and around a set of sharp curves down into a bog of musty old woods and up again to a straight stretch beside fields of weeds turned golden in the sunset and beyond the fields stood the house.

"Where is this?" Glenda asked. "Where have we got to?"

"A friend's place."

"What friend?"

"Nobody you know, girl. Nobody you need to know."

The house stood close to the road but lower. The road set even with the porch light. The house was a mussed white color and had numerous levels. At the top level there were those attic windows that fit onto the house like eyeballs squinting to keep a close unfriendly watch on all things. The roof was groomed into points in three or four spots with black metal items perched on the points. Many many lights were on inside.

There was a yard light, a big white globe on a pole. A bunch of vehicles parked near the light. There were pickup trucks, one with a wood pigpen on back, and another loaded with sacks of feed. The other vehicles were all cars splotched with dust.

Red parked among the others.

I could see folks in the house holding cards under a cloud of smoke. I could see hands shaking dice. I could see drinks raised and dollar bills tossed down.

He said, "Back in a flash. And y'all don't need to hear no music—this battery won't take it."

She and me did sit there no better than bumps on a log as dark fell over us and nothing did get spoken between us until the dark became full black and the bug chants loud.

"Sorry," she said. "I should've got a lot smarter to his

tricks by now. I guess I'm stupid."

"No you're not."

"I should've got smarter to his tricks."

"You are, Glenda. You are smarter to his tricks."

"You think?"

"Yeah. I mean, you knew he'd do *something* to us, didn't you? You knew he'd pull *some* shit."

"I had a hunch."

I could see him inside, track his oiled bump of hair as he worked through the crowd to a table and slid to a seat.

"Glenda, he said to me that he *loved* you."

"Did he? Oh, hon." She laid her head back and closed her eyes. She reached over and squeezed my knee. "Think what *I* think about that."

HE came back to us broke and wanted her shirt for a new start. He did not come alone. She and me had fallen asleep, nudged together in the cab of the truck, and the words he spoke were slow in making sense to us.

"Shake a leg, Glenda. Get your ass out here."

The man with him made a stout shape in the dark, standing beside Red between the truck and the yard light. A cigarette glowed at his mouth. A hat with a cowboy brim rode the top of him.

Red said, "I'm tellin' you it's worth somethin'."

"You said that. You keep sayin' it."

"'Cause it's so."

"Says you."

"I bet you dig it. I bet you will."

"You ain't hardly won a bet since you showed your face."

"Luck turns, don't it? Mine's turnin' now."

Me and Glenda fell from the truck, sleepy yet and dizzy from missing supper. She pushed me back with her hand, halted me, and stepped forward.

"What is it you want?"

"See?" Red said. "Nice, huh?"

The man said, "I reckon."

"So why don't you give me a ten-spot on it?"

"Ten? Naw."

"Glenda, raise your arms and do a little spin. It's real silk, man. Guaranteed. *Did you hear me?* I said do a little spin."

The man said, "I can see it. I can see it fine."

"I need me a ten-spot, dig?"

"Nope." The man stepped over and rubbed his fingers on the collar of Glenda's shirt. She would not look at him. "I'll go seven."

"That's gettin' near on to ten—why don't you go ten?"

"I'll go *seven*. That's the end of hagglin'."

Red put his arm around Glenda and walked her behind the truck to where I stood. He held her clamped in close under his arm, almost a headlock. "You gotta give it," he said. "I gotta have it."

She turned white. She could not have turned whiter even with disease to rinse her down, but she kept her chin raised. I could see she trembled.

"You . . . will not . . . do this to me."

"Wrong." He slapped a claw at her neck, pushing

her head back, pinching her windpipe. A rattling noise came from her, the rattle of words that did not live past her throat to be heard. His free claw unbuttoned the silk. "I ain't askin', witch. Did it sound like I was askin'?" As he pulled the shirt open he bent to her bra, pulled one half low and smooched her nipple. His tongue licked a circle. He smooched twice. "Titty suck for luck."

She spun away with her arms crossed over her chest and hunkered behind the truck. Her bare skin seemed to glow. I followed Red as he carried the silk to the stout man. When he passed the silk over I tried to snatch it back. The man pulled it away from me and held it over my head.

"Best put a leash on your pup."

"Fat boy," Red muttered, and grabbed me by the chest of my striped shirt and lifted, lifted with power, popping all the buttons free. "Go sit your ass in the truck with your witch. Got that? *Sit*. And don't start lookin' for me 'til you see me comin'."

SHE and me did take off from the gambling house but not towards anyplace we knew of for certain. She and me walked back the way we thought we came. She carried her heels in her hands and went barefoot to feel our way along that skinny streak of dirt in such deep darkness. She took small steps forward and tapped the ground ahead with her toes and the feel of dirt on her toes meant the path laid under us yet and we would shuffle that much further.

"Be careful of ruts," she said. "Don't twist an ankle."

I gave up my shirt to Glenda though the buttons had been burst from the cloth and none were left to button. I had seen her nipple good when Red had him a smooch for luck, and she used my shirt to cover that section of herself. She wore my shirt over her front, her arms through the sleeves backwards, covering her to the throat, though her back was entirely bare skin but for the bra strap. The clearest thing I did see in such dark was the shine of her back.

"Stay close."

"Let's hold hands."

"Yes, let's, hon."

We were going our own way from Red but very slow. On the straight stretch past the fields our pace became faster, some, though not much. She felt ahead with her toes and pulled me along behind her and often we both sucked loud breaths together when we heard the same alarming noise. So many creatures make noise in the country at night. They made noises that meant something among themselves and could be they meant something about us. We both were town-raised and many many of the noises in the weeds or high limbs or near distance made us pause and stand very very still like standing still hid us from things that could hunt in woods at night.

"Keep a tight hold on my hand."

The noise *we* made was slaps. Mosquitoes had us slapping at our skins the way dust gets beat from a rug. Slap slap slap we went but still the bugs found bare skin and drilled on us for blood wherever no slaps hit. A few times Glenda also leaked out a noise like a sob had jumped up inside her but she straightaway swallowed it silent.

"Mom, are we sure where this goes?"

"Not really. Stay close."

The path curved and went down to the smelly boggy woods. That area smelled like the musty basement to a building that was not there. The trees there grew bigger and closer to the path. It seemed to me that such a path might contain ambushes and a good place to set some would be in the boggy stretch.

"Let me in front—I got a blade."

"Sold. Don't try to go too fast."

No light from anywhere showed to help in the bog. It was pure dark all over down there but I did imagine I could kind of see the shape of my blade poking the space ahead of us to clear the path. I might have stabbed anything. Glenda kept close behind by linking a finger through a belt loop on my jeans. Further along the bog smell became like a smell grown so sweet it had turned yucky. The path felt thicker under my feet, mushy, and tree limbs had reached across the path to make a low ceiling.

She tugged at my belt loop.

"Stomp your feet now and then."

"What for?"

"For snakes to hear."

Step step stomp.

Step step stomp.

The path rose from the bog and turned and became regular dirt again. The normal woods smelled so fresh. We did walk on and on in the same order, her finger hooked to me, my blade in my hand, feeling our way along the path the way blind folks cross a new street.

I heard the paws thudding and something tinkled but the dogs were invisible until they stopped to snarl just one jump from our ankles. I could see a light on in a house set back from the road. The dogs barked angry bullying barks. Their snorts of breath puffed over my ankles.

She got right up against my back and clung.

The dogs made practice moves for attacking.

I was ready to stab but there were two.

I said, "Why don't they call their goddamn dogs?"

"Country folks seem to want them this way."

"I'll kill one for sure."

We shuffled backwards, her behind me clinging, the shoes in her hands tapping my shoulders. We kept the dogs to my front and eased forward on the path and the dogs followed, hungry hungry hungry to make a meal of us to hear them tell it. Nobody stirred from the farmhouse. I kept the blade pointed down ready to plunge and thought fast thoughts about big white teeth tearing the meat of me and enjoying the taste.

"Don't kick—they'll get your foot."

The dogs never became clear. Fair-sized from their sounds, the scraping of claws, the huffing. We eased away on the path the way pissdrops ease down your leg after a punch to the tummy. She clung but good. I'd become ready to know the feel of that thin bright blade slicing into something that breathed and bothered us. Feel how it cut towards the heart of something alive.

"They're stopping, hon. They're pulling back."

"Must be this is the end of their land."

"I don't hear anybody callin' them."

"Let's go faster."

We then hustled along the path with our pace picked up, taking big blind steps in the dark, but acting like we could see.

AT the filling station she peeked in the window on the back door, then said, "We need a phone, Shug."

"Who'll you call?"

"You know who."

"Reckon he'll come?"

She pointed at that old back door on that sagging filling station.

"Phone."

I swiped us a pack of smokes, also, and we hunkered in the blackest shadows outdoors to wait. The smokes were the wrong make but okay in a pinch.

"Shug, don't you think he's sort of cute?"

My striped shirt kept sliding from her white white shoulders and she kept raising it back. The shadows we sat in were against the west wall of the station. This sort of smoke did actually taste more to my liking than the brand she trained me on but I never did say that.

"No."

"He's not cute?"

"I sure wouldn't say so."

"In his way, I mean."

"Huh-uh."

"But he looks, like, distinguished. Right?"

"The best thing about him I can see is his car."

"I think he is, in his own way, *real* dashing."

I lit me a smoke from the butt of the first.

"I know you do."

HE thought to bring sandwiches. Steak sandwiches that had sweet onion strands cooked limp and brown and laid on top. The sauce I could not see and did not know but tasted near wonderful. He had spruced to fetch us, shaped his wisps of hair, shaved and splashed his face with that sailor smell. He looked at me, who had no shirt, and her, who had only mine to wear backwards. He glanced several times before he spoke: "Just tell me what you want me to know."

"Oh," she went, "could we just leave it alone?"

"Yes'm. That's ofttimes the best course."

My body felt tired from gooseflesh outside to the bone inside, but also starved to where my brain staggered. I tore away at the sandwich before I got it all unwrapped, chomped teeth into the steak, and liked it. I liked it so much. I liked it so loud they both turned and grinned at me. I liked the sandwich down to crumbs in no time, and I liked the crumbs for a minute or so.

She said, "This is awful good of you."

"I'm glad you called."

"Glad?"

"Well . . . see . . . I've had your smile in my mind for days and days now, and it wouldn't get out."

Her answer was not a word, only a sound, a murmur, a pleased murmur. Her next words were, "Is that bourbon I smell?"

"Yup. Bottle on the floorboard, there."

"Oh. Yeah. Mind?"

"It's meant to be drunk, ma'am."

The Thunderbird moved along at a calm pace. The windows all were down before long and the scents of the thickets beside the road blew in on us, blew out, then more blew in. Crickets had their racket going, their loud one-two noise, sounding like a giant squeaky seesaw. Now and then the lights skimmed a dark spot and eyes reflected.

I guess eating slid me towards sleep, there, in the backseat, but I heard certain things: "Gamblin' turns him noodles in the head."

And: "I was married when I went there. He had a legal scrape to pay for, and I had a aunt in Covington."

And: "The Baron—he had one of those kind of wives who don't much cotton to havin' me around."

When the T-bird stopped, the stopping moved me and eased me mostly awake. The T-bird was in the cemetery, parked in the drive by our house. My bare gut was chilled from the late-night air. I laid still.

She said, "I know he knows. He always has known, but we stayed married. He knows, but he never says it, not exactly."

"So the man just broods on it."

"Since I came home I felt way way in debt to him."

"A debt paid in full, I'd say. A couple of times over."

I opened my eyes then, and saw they sat close together.

"Glenda, I'm chilly. Time to go in."

"You go on, hon."

"You come, too."

"We're talkin', Shug. You go on."

"You come, too."

"Huh-uh, hon."

"Listen, if he touches you, I'll knock fire from his ass."

"You hush. Hush up. This man has been *so* nice to us. *Go.*"

I went. It was late and I went because I was sleepy and she sent me. Once inside I stared out the screen. They rolled the windows up against the cool. I could not go to bed, go to bed with her out there, out there with him, so I laid over the kitchen table, the tilting table, my head on my arms.

Later I looked and the T-bird windows had clouded.

When the daybreak birds started their regular loud singalong I looked again and could not see their heads.

I fell asleep, facedown on the table, and the sun was up when I woke to her sitting across from me. My shirt was barely on her and her bra was in her hands.

"*Honey?* Shuggie, honey. Just forget what you think you saw me do, and keep this in mind—I love *you.*"

13

DAMNED FOOL THING OF THEM to set a sign *there."* Granny said that standing in the afternoon heat smoking a long cigarette she'd lit to the side of the tip. She stood there not moving her feet but waving like horseweed in a breeze. She had the slit-eyed look of a cowpoke scanning a hot prairie. Her cigarette burned along at an angle.

Carl said, "It's a stop sign, Ma."

Him and me and her looked down at the sign. She had knocked the sign flat. We had been throwing newspapers and she for some reason wanted to go in reverse but the refreshments had got to her and she ran the station wagon over the curb and square into the sign.

"I ain't about to mess my bloomers over it," she said. She let loose with the sound called cackling. She slapped at her knee. When she spoke her lips sucked into her mouth and blew out with the words. "Damned fools set a sign *there*, they got to take what they get."

"It's a corner, Ma. Stop signs go at corners."

Granny told the road to obey her wishes when she was drunk and seemed to think it would. She wished the road would turn *now* or add another lane *now* or raise up and shake itself clean of other traffic. Strangers weren't sure she was drunk, but I knew. Granny got braggish when drunk. She got swole up about herself. When she took to bragging on her thoughts and notions it was time to jump from the station wagon and walk or brace for a crash.

Carl said, "We best stick it back up. Those folks over there saw it happen."

"Might be I'll just prance over there and whup the lot of 'em 'til they mind their *own damn business*."

"No, no ass-whuppin', Ma."

She stood beside the station wagon that was loaded with rolled papers, and the engine still ran so the wagon wobbled behind her and spit smoke from the tailpipe.

"I b'lieve I could do it."

"I believe you're goin' to jail if we don't fix this sign pretty quick."

"There ain't no jail gonna hold me, son."

"Just stay there!" Carl wore regular tan-type pants with two full legs of cloth. He wanted his crater hidden in public. His walk had plenty of hop yet in it as he walked over to the sign. "Give me a hand, Shug."

I did then tell him what I had noted already.

"The sign's bent all to hell, Carl."

"It is, is it?"

"It's bent bad as a horseshoe. Down low there. A horseshoe ain't goin' to stand up straight."

Carl leaned on me a little and I smelled his usual day-long smell of beer and cigarettes. His head hair had grown to touch his ears and he was trying for a mustache but still had a ways to go. His weight was not bad leaning on me and we both looked at the sign. He said, "I don't reckon we can fix that."

"No way."

"Then di di mau, baby. Di di mau. I'll drive."

* * *

TO make the paper-throwing fun we invented a contest. Carl drove sitting slouched at an angle, his bad leg raised partly onto the front seat so he could twist about and work the pedals with his good leg, the left. He kept a can of beer on his lap and kept the radio playing loud. Granny leaned from the passenger-side front window and I did lean from the window behind her, and we flung papers at the right addresses, aiming for the front porches or sidewalks. A porch hit meant five points and a sidewalk two.

"You got to aim more," I said.

"I might aim upside your head."

"Don't be a sore loser, Granny."

"I ain't lost yet, fatty."

She had to call the way for Carl to drive because he did not know every house on the route. She would call out, "This one," and me or her would throw the paper and Carl would keep the score tallied for us. The houses were of all types except the poorest sort of houses like ours where it seemed the news was of no concern to hardly anybody. Some of the richer houses had fabulous deep tangles of bushes and shit framing their front porches and stray papers could get lost in such fabulous tangles. When throws like that happened I had to get out and hunt the paper. I had to burrow however deep into the bushes the paper had fallen. Some bush needles didn't feel nice on my skin, and some scratched, but none drew blood so it flowed.

I'd come back scratched and say, "Throw straight,

Granny. Or don't throw."

"If I was as big a sissy as you, boy, I wouldn't let on."

I don't know how many papers we threw but it seemed a full load. Folks were out watering lawns and nodded at us. Kids smacked plastic balls with fat plastic bats. Women crouched in flower beds and stirred the dirt with trowels. At some houses the sounds of supper being cooked carried to the street and reached me.

At the end of the route Carl called out the score.

"Well, you *oughta* be able to beat your old granny," she said.

"I did, too."

Carl drove on into the cemetery and up to the house. He hit the brakes and turned the radio low. The house was open to the screen door but no vehicle sat out front.

"You *oughta* be able to."

"I *am*."

"It'd be pretty god-awful sad if you *couldn't* beat me."

"But I can, Granny. I did. And I'll do it more next time."

Carl had started singing with a song on the radio but looked back at me and laughed a couple of times.

She said, "Why don't you get on out? You get on out now, and run to your momma. See if *Momma's* got a *cookie* for you."

"I believe I will. Later, Carl."

* * *

SOMEBODY bleeding had whirled and whirled in the kitchen. Dishes had crashed about and made a mess. The blood had whirled odd spots and streaks onto the stove, the walls, the floor, the ceiling. The kind of plates we had that could be broken were busted on the floor. The radio played olden rhyming rock'n roll songs. A leg was gone from the table and the table bent over, the top touched to the floor like it kneeled to beg.

Our habit had got to be that whenever Jimmy Vin came calling I sat on the roof of the shed to keep a watch out. I never could be all the way sure which exact vehicle I needed to spot, which set of wheels spelled doom. I watched for Red in every car, every truck, looking for that oiled bump of hair, those big arms.

I pulled my blade out.

Other times Jimmy Vin scooped us into the T-bird and off we went to places he enjoyed. Him and her laughed together a bunch. They smiled and smiled except when something made her nervous and she ducked. He enjoyed food and we went to places to eat, mainly. One place on the lake had noodles that were like tubes, and slices of a sausage I never had before in tomato sauce. Me and Glenda loved the food so much, smacked and smacked our lips, until he finally said, "Too light on the garlic. A little too much sugar in the sauce. Otherwise, pretty fair."

Water gurgled in the sink. Some streaks of blood seemed to yet be moving down the sides of things. That music played that I never did care to hear and I turned it off.

He always had been happy to spend and spending

put that glow in her eyes. He never looked at the amounts on menus, just the choices. He often asked for extra touches from the kitchen for his food. "Something as simple as a slice of Bermuda onion added to a burger makes the burger two stars better." The tips he left caused waitresses to follow us clear out to the parking lot wishing us well.

Hands had posted bloody signs along the wall and into the hall. The signs were smeared. Her room was down the hall. Her room with the bed was down the hall.

They right away started kissing in front of me.

I flicked the blade open and creeped along.

A sheet from the bed had landed in the hall.

There were certain things he wanted his way. He wanted her hair worked over and puffed into that hard round style, a hair helmet, plenty of spray. He thought lots of makeup looked better than less. "I guess my tastes are set," he said. "You are a doll."

Clumps of long raven hair lay on the sheet, clumps like a cat fight leaves in a corner.

The man wore neckties awful regular for around here.

She took to bringing him up in talk when we were alone.

"Don't you think he'd make a good daddy?"

"I don't care much for daddies. Daddies stink."

The bedroom didn't look that bad except for the things tipped over. I eased into the room and looked for the bodies. I figured there'd be bodies. I never had figured I'd be the one who'd have to find the bodies.

This other time, I hunkered on the T-bird hood and kept the watch for them and did not hear too much mumbling and thumping from the house. The sky was in that gray mood, that gray mood on a hot day that might mean rain is on the way, rain and nasty weather, or maybe nothing is coming except more gray on a hot hot afternoon. When a breeze kicked up birds went for cover in the cemetery trees. Those two had their arms over each other as they strolled outside. When he drove off she switched her hugs back to me. Now she had hugs for me. I wiggled from her hugs and shoved her arms away.

"Oh, Shug, do you hate me? Say you don't hate me."

"Quit it, Glenda."

"Say it. Say it for me, hon."

"Do I seem like I hate you?"

"But you could. You could hate me, and I want to know."

"I don't fuckin' hate you!"

I pulled the screen door open and stood there, one foot in the house, my eyes raised to the gray windy sky.

"You didn't need to *yell* it."

I let the door slap behind me, then turned and faced her with the screen between us.

"Button your shirt straight."

The bodies weren't in the bedroom. So I checked the TV room where it seemed nothing at all had happened.

The table leg had landed behind the fridge. I picked

it up. Blood and skin stuck to the heavy end. I carried the table leg to the john and stood over the tiny pond. I used my blade to scrape the table leg. It was a sliver of meat ripped loose from some part of a person. Maybe a lip. Maybe a ear. Almost a eyelid but probably not. The meat looked sad with no face to frame it. The skin came off like goo and as the goo hit the water I flushed.

Back in the kitchen I saw the sink had a boot in it.

Water gurgled over the boot. The boot had white eagle wings.

I about collapsed.

I rinsed the table leg in the sink. I raised the table from where it kneeled and put the leg back where it belonged so the table could stand. I got the broom and a mop and a bucket of water and a sponge. I started sweeping the broken dishes. I picked up the dishes that weren't broken. I had almost swept the floor clean when I saw the black skillet under a chair. Strange stuff clung to the skillet and I bent for a look. I plucked the strip of meat off the skillet with my fingers pinched and spotted hairs growing from it.

The hairs were red.

I went back to the john and the hairs waved and waved as they swirled down.

I followed the blood around the kitchen with a sponge. The blood had in some places splashed out pictures. Mostly faces or maps. I rubbed and rubbed and rubbed. I stood on the stove to scrub swipes of blood that had spurted to the ceiling. I found drops to scrub all over. They got into the strangest places. I rubbed and swept and rubbed and mopped. Then I went to work on the blood signs posted in the hall.

At the sink I tipped the water from the boot and the water poured out bloody. I scrubbed all around the sink. I carried the boot into the yard and over to the shed. I climbed to the dark rafters of the shed and stuck the boot in the farthest dark place.

I put everything away. I made myself a baloney and mayonnaise sandwich for supper. I sat in front of the TV and watched whatever it was that was on. I watched a long time. I found some chip crumbs in a bag and ate them.

She came in while I was watching a show. I heard her walk all about the house. I heard her feet moving in the hall. I heard her in the kitchen. I didn't make a sound.

I knew she stood in the doorway watching me a long time before she spoke.

"What's goin' on, Shug?"

"I already ate."

Not long after that she still stood there looking and he joined her and she said, "He already ate."

"He did, did he?"

"What'd you find to eat?"

I turned to look at them and he had a blue bulge popped out on his forehead. A fat black lump had risen under his left eye and made the eye squinch. His nostrils had that crust left by bloody noses. She looked shook up and pale and her hair did not lay calmly on her head. They both had dirty sections at their knees and filthy hands.

"Baloney."

He pointed into the kitchen and gave her a big-eyed confused look and she shrugged at him two or three times.

"Baloney?" she said. "That's all? Well, then, I'll bet you're ready for your snack, aren't you, hon?"

I turned my face back to the TV. I watched whatever was on. Some show.

"I could use a snack."

14

NORMAL DAYS SPUN WITH a different wobble for a while. Sometimes I thought the house shivered. The regular things happened but they did not seem so regular, and things that weren't regular butted in on each day. A house that shivered threw everything off. Jimmy Vin stayed away and left her alone with her thoughts and she stayed drunk. Each day she started out expecting him, trying to smile, waiting, more and more fidgety, but he would not show. Before lunch she'd take her silvery thermos into the bedroom and lay there and now and then ask me did I see the Thunderbird circling around.

"No. Quit askin'."

The cemetery gave me something to do. Plots with weeds I never had kneeled down and pulled got snatched baldheaded practically. Some of the oldest white markers in the olden stretch of cemetery ground had fallen before my time and been propped back up by piles of smaller flat rocks. Most of the headstones were propped up tilted. I studied on the smaller flat rocks and how they were stacked, then built fresh piles that shoved the markers up more straight. I built the piles my own way, just so. The names still could not be read but the blurred headstones stood prouder. On some days I kicked the piles away so everything fell, then built the headstones up straight all over again.

"Quit askin'."

I wondered if Red was laid in the dirt and worms

were already eating the soft parts of him. Eyeballs, lips, ears, tongue. Armies of worms gobbling his soft parts. Worms wiggling in and out of his meat. Or were the worms still crawling their way underground towards him? Was he buried deep wrapped in something stout that slowed the march of the gobbling worms? Or could be him and her had just pulled over above a steep ravine and rolled him down into the scrub oak and trash weeds so he'd come to rest in the open air where the big snorty hungry animals sniffed over to him and chewed the best meat of him away first. And when the big animals had gorged full, the worms would march in wiggling for the leavings on his bones.

"Goddammit, no! Quit askin'."

15

THE FIRST PERSON TO MISS RED and say so was Basil. Basil had been stuck for most of a week in the town jail because of a petty deed he did not care to talk about, and a day after they let him out he fell by our house when Glenda was in a weaving way and staggered around the kitchen drunk as hell. She opened all the drawers for a look but never found what she thought she hunted and let the drawers hang open. She muttered pieces of several sentences and bounced from the walls. She had not tended to her grooming much for days, or changed shirts, and looked about as far from good as she ever could.

He said, "Poor gal—she's missin' him bad as me."

"She's drunk."

The time was sunset and the sky was finger-painted with swirls of three or four colors, but the big splashes were pink.

"She's hurtin', Shug. Really hurtin'."

"She didn't eat no supper."

Glenda soon staggered right up to us but went past like we were stumps and weaved her way on into the TV room. We watched as she reached the old gray couch and flopped out flat.

"She's hurtin' too bad to eat."

Basil stood there with his hands on his hips, giving sad little shakes of his head. He wore a starchy white shirt and black pants like for churchgoing and had shaved. His hair was cut tidy and combed. He had driven over in a rackety white Mustang that needed a tune-up to put the pistons in step with each other again.

I said, "You look all freshened up from jail."

"I turned me a new leaf in there." Basil grinned sort of bashful, then nodded. "I set my brain to doin' jumpin' jacks and shit. Made it run laps, do a few chin-ups. I've got to get thinkin' right—I've even swore off dope."

"You have? Since when?"

"Tomorrow's gonna make two days. That's not countin' the six days in jail. You can't fairly count them."

"Huh-uh," I went. "You can't." Glenda was asleep with her chin down and her mouth sagged open. Her breaths honked through her nose. "Swore off for good?"

"Swore off 'til I find my partner. I ain't become no square citizen just yet. I ain't sayin' that. But I can't hunt Red if I'm fucked up constantly to where my brain's stuck in low gear."

"I imagine he's drifted off somewhere scallybippin'."

"Well now, Red might sure 'nough go out scallybippin' for a couple of weeks without tellin' *her*, but not without tellin' *me*." Basil took a smoke pack from his shirt pocket and tapped cigs loose for us both. He had a hefty gray lighter that clanged open and threw a big flame. "Red ain't pulled nothin' much important without me there to take his back since about seventh grade, man. Since your age."

There were laughing voices in the bone orchard.

Kids with dogs chased other kids and dogs over grave-humps and around tombstones and in amongst the old resting trees. They ran each other down in the twilight and tagged to make somebody else It. The dogs chased any kid who ran. Over the way a mother called and called for her kid to come in now, your daddy says *right now*, it's getting dark. The kids laughed louder than the mother's call.

I said, "Things ain't goin' good around here."

He even smelled like a new and different Basil. He smelled of soap and aftershave and I think baby powder. His ear hairs had been clipped.

"Red take much with him?"

"Got me."

"Let's look."

Basil moved on down the hall to the bedroom and looked in at the mess. Her underwear laid on the floor where he could see. Dirty clothes and dirty dishes sat around. Ashtrays were full to the rim. Smells had begun to rally in there. Nobody changed the sheets lately and sweat and spilled stuff had created patterns.

"Jesus, kid—your momma is fallin' all apart."

"It's not goin' good."

"Ain't love a motherfucker? She's in pieces. Crushed to pieces. Makes me want to cry, man."

I shuffled back towards the TV room and he came along. He dealt us each new smokes and threw the flame. He sighed every time he blew out. The sputter of Glenda's lips grew louder. A couple of times she shook up from the couch like a line was hooked to her chest and getting jerked.

"I best roll her on her face," I said. "Make sure she won't drown there on the couch."

"Ugh. Pew! I'll leave you to it, ol' son. I reckon I gotta be somewhere else—best get you a bucket."

"Got one under the sink."

He moved to the screen door and I shadowed him. His eyes looked around pretty sharp. He even stood with better posture now.

"Basil, I've got to say, that is really somethin' about you quittin' dope."

"It *is*, ain't it? It *is* really somethin'. Course, not havin' any on hand is a big, big help."

Those kids and dogs were yet out there scurrying across the dead, making their happy sounds. Fireflies hung flashing in the air and thumb bats swooped to eat them.

"I better go get her on her face."

"Sure as hell sounds like it, kid."

I fetched the trash bucket and rolled Glenda over. Her mouth was stuck together by dry spit and her sticky lips split apart slow. Her eyelids trembled but did not open. When the jerks and sputters started I slid her head to the edge and held the bucket beneath her chin. Each heave made her bounce on the couch. She heaved and heaved. All she held down in her did soon come up and out and I caught each mouthful in the trash bucket and tried and tried and tried not to see any sights I couldn't forget.

OUT BESIDE THOSE TOMBSTONES under that hot sun only the fake flowers lasted. The fake flowers turned lighter-colored as they baked but stayed somewhat stiff atop paling green stems. Actual real true flowers strangled in such heat, choked, shriveled up limp and twisted, and soon came to look like garbage heaped ugly on the graves.

I rolled the wheelbarrow all along the cemetery rows, looking at the popular graves, the graves with piled bouquets, and raked up the ruined flowers that were due to be burned. This was before lunch. The sun had not nearly got to full strength and a slow breeze came and went. I rolled the wheelbarrow straight past the forgotten dead as no flowers gathered on them. The forgotten dead were not all from long ago, while some of the most popular dead had been gone a hundred years or better but still knew folks who came around to see them with bunches of flowers.

The fire barrel stood out behind the tractor shed. It was a big rusty thing. I started with burning paper, then dropped in handfuls of summer-white grass, twigs, and limbs. The fire built fast and was soon ready for business. The flames jumped up high and wiggling from the barrel. I pitched flowers on the fire. I tossed the ruined true flowers and some of the fakes that were past faking they were flowers and started being plastic trash. The true flowers stunted the flames and the fakes fed them.

When I returned to the fire rolling another load Glenda sat there on a house chair holding her silvery thermos. She wore a blue dress that was meant to be worn of an evening to somewhere swank and lively. Her feet were bare. Her hair looked to be a little bit brushed.

"I do believe your *muscles* are startin' to show, hon."

"Are they?"

"Up there high on your arms. You've got nice *strong* shoulders."

I tipped the wheelbarrow load of ruined flowers at her feet. She touched the heap with her toes. She picked up something with yellow petals.

"You reckon this was a rose?"

"Burn those while I fetch more."

Next time I fed the fire a few limbs before I fed it more flowers. I got the flames to snap and jump way up from the barrel. She and me both stood there tossing in flowers.

She said, "When you see the judge you can put it off on Red. You can put it all on him."

Some of the flowers came with ribbons that said things on them. "Blessed Forever," "Sleeping in His Arms," "Beloved." I dangled a ribbon into the fire and held it as the flames ate towards my fingers.

"Won't that get the law to come snoopin' around lookin' for him? Askin' people stuff?"

"Oh, God." She sat down hard and the chair groaned. I heard the thermos open. "I am so stupid anymore. I am so stupid. Stupid in every direction."

As the ribbon burned to the size of a stamp I let it fall

into the barrel. She made noises sitting there, noises that go with worries, or maybe fright.

She said, "There won't be any money anymore."

I guess I rolled on out and about the graves gathering another load. I took my time rolling up and down the ranks. Three or four customers came around laying fresh flowers as I went along. I kept clear of them and dawdled. I took so much time dawdling she came out barefoot across the bone orchard to join me. She sidled close and threw an arm around my shoulders.

"I'm about to get right again, Shug. Believe me. I'm just about to put myself back together the way I was."

"When?"

"A certain day is goin' to come."

"What certain day?"

"Hon, hon, hon—it's not a *certain* certain day. It's *one* of these days."

"You're boiled."

A cop car screamed past on the hard road, cherry-top churning in daylight, leading two unmarked cars over the hill and into something.

I rolled the next batch of trash flowers back to the fire barrel and she followed. The dry white grass felt like whisker stubble underfoot and made a scratchy sound when stepped on. She followed me quietly and when we reached the barrel, I told her, "Go on, sit in your chair. Sit."

"Your muscles," she said. "Just there your muscles shined, hon. They showed good."

The fire burned on until far past time for lunch. The

fire, too, got hungry and limp and fell down to a low tired flame. The smoke grew too thin to mark a trail in the air, but the smoke had already worked into my hair and clothes so the smell from the fire barrel came along to anywhere I stood. My hands purely stunk.

"You know, you can go on in."

"No, hon. Huh-uh. I feel better helpin'."

For quite a while it went like that. It went like that until we both saw the Thunderbird turning into our long curled drive through the cemetery. She became still on her chair, a rock, her eyes locked on the green green color and white-ringed tires. The shine from the sun made the car glow extra. Jimmy Vin drove towards us at a low speed, his head stiff on his neck, eyes forward, both hands on the wheel. He parked beside the shed facing the barrel.

He sat there and she sat where she sat and they both stared. Her face did not move. Her face did not show a single ripple. Her eyes seemed not to blink. Neither of them smiled or melted or sang out.

I stirred the fire with a stick.

Next time I looked he was standing beside his car. She stood, too. She stood a little slumped, but she stood. He took the first step, then stopped. She tried a step his way and stopped. Their stares held and held and held, then broke, and both came loose and ran together. Their meat smacked together to make a smooching sound. They stood hugged together next to the fire barrel without trying any words, only little purrs and sniffles and gulps. His hands flowed around feeling of her.

She said the first words: "I had just about got over you."

"I was afraid of that."

HIS return and a night of sleep knocked her parts back together. Once knocked back together she looked around and faced it that household things had not been getting done and the house had become a stinking mess. Lots of little things hadn't been done, and dishes and laundry, big things, had been piled high instead of done.

Glenda woke early that morning and seemed to have been rearranged in her sleep into someone peppy.

"Coffee. Coffee first, my sweet, then we'll get after all this mess."

Dishes stood in splayed stacks around the sink. Peas and macaroni and bread crusts had gathered in the drain and dammed the water so it rose greasy and topped with food bits to the crest of the sink. The faucet could not be turned on without causing a flood.

"You have to root in the mess for a cup," I said. "Find one, see, then take it to the bathtub to clean it."

"Yup. Yup. It seems it's come to that."

The morning sun shined through a sky blown clear of clouds and dewdrops on the grass caught the early light to sparkle while birds fluttered about being loudmouthed and busy the way birds are at the start of a day. We drank coffee and looked out the screen at all this, and even the tombstones looked to have been buffed overnight.

"Well, hon, I guess right off we need to empty the trash."

"There sure is plenty."

We carried the trash to the shed and I stomped the bags to fit into the cans. Stuff squeezed from the bags in drools as I stomped, and I had to scrape my shoes.

"I said I'd get right. Didn't I say it?"

"You said it."

She dragged her bare feet along the grass and dew splattered on her skin until her feet shined. She wore shorts that were not too motherly. They fit on her mighty scenic. She had taken a white shirt of Red's and knotted the tails above her belly button and rolled the sleeves above her elbows. Her smell was back as good as ever, which was great. She moved about real peppy, all limber and wiggly, that way of moving called sashay.

She said, "Our house ain't much, but I'll let you in on something—I *know* it ain't much."

"We should make the house just one color."

"No dough for paint."

I smacked her on the butt, a pretty crisp smack. Her mouth opened in the shape to say "Oh!" but didn't say it. Her hands went back and rubbed the smacked spot on her butt. She gave me this look over her shoulder, mouth still shaped to say "Oh!" but not saying it, and rubbed her butt slower so the cloth shifted with each rub and the hem worked up a nudge higher on her rump.

It seemed I heard a giggle.

"Okay. Okay now, hon. I guess I do have a swat comin' to me, the way I've been lately."

I bent to smack her butt another and she clenched so

my hand came down on a nice firm round rump and the smack sound was cute.

"Now, that'll do! That's enough."

The smack had sent her flinching onto tippy-toes, her whole body flexed taut, and this flinch posture drew those shorts higher. Those shorts were not too motherly to start with. The shorts rode higher on her ass, then stopped.

I said, "Only teasin'."

Her fingers went back and pulled the shorts lower. She laughed then for sure. It was a clear and plain laugh. She swept her feet along raking through the dew and led back to the kitchen.

"If I wash that means you dry."

"I dig," I said.

We went to work on the dirty dishes. Slosh and scrape and scrape and slosh, rinse and dry. Thumbnails had to pry under some stains to chip them off certain dishes. She stood there at the sink scrubbing, leaning her weight from one leg to the other and back again. Now and then she danced a dance something like the twist. Dishwater splashed on the white shirt she wore and made spots you could kind of see through.

I don't know. I could not say exactly, but somehow the dish towel fell and both my hands flew to her ass. Both hands landed on her sweet sashaying rump in those short-shorts. She stood like a statue. She made a sound that was likely a gasp. Her skin felt so fine and curved as my hands slid up under the hem on those shorts. She did not move a twitch. She was a statue. My hands went higher and ran around front and creeped inside her panties and rubbed pussy hair. I guess my head simmered when I felt pussy hair.

"No. No, Shug. No."

Her shorts were yanked down her legs, undies too, and I fell back a pace to look, and while I looked a wave of something new slapped me, slapped all thoughts from my head and only left me with heat. I sprang back onto her, tousled her pussy hair, pulled a finger through the damp strange furrow, felt her sag. My hands pulled free and climbed for a rough feel under her shirt. Both hands filled and I tried to spin her to get my lips on there, for titty-suck.

That's when she slumped to the floor and away from my hands. She landed with a thump. She sat on the floor, head down, raven hair fallen around her face. She sat that way for quite a spell. Slowly she worked her shorts on again.

"What on earth are you doin'?"

"Havin' a feel of you."

She shoved up and stood and pushed me away.

"This *can't* happen. You *can't* paw me, Shug. You *can't*. They say it's wrong, and . . . and you just can't."

"Everybody else does."

She edged away to the tilted table. She did not sit but did light a smoke. Her shorts were not pulled up level and were slung low below her belly button so she still made a picture.

"Everybody else does not."

We stood that way a good while without words.

"I only wanted a feel of it. Like everybody else."

"You're *not* everybody else."

"Should I mix you your tea? Huh?"

"Good Lord, no. Take a cold bath. Take a *long* cold bath, then get outside. Mow or something. That's it. Take a cold, cold bath, then *get*."

I was out in the cemetery on the tractor cruising about more than mowing and I heard a horn toot and looked to the hard road and saw Basil whipping past in the white Mustang. He gave me the finger the way friends do. He was going somewhere else in a hurry and I cruised on until I heard tires squeal to a stop. Slender smoke whiffs rose from the sudden tire tracks. The Mustang clanged gears and slammed backwards my way awful fast until the tires squealed to another stop. Basil flew out leaving the motor on and the door hanging open. He ran to the rock wall that surrounded the bone orchard and leaped over it.

As he closed on me I switched the tractor off.

He said, "Where in hell'd you get that shirt?"

"This one?"

"Where did you get that fuckin' shirt?"

"The house."

"The house?"

"Up at the house."

"That is Red's shirt, fat boy. Goddammit. Goddammit. Since when is it Red lets you wear his stuff?"

"He don't."

"I know he don't. I do know that. Most generally he'd bust you in the fuckin' mouth for even touchin' his stuff. Whip your ass 'til butter squeezes from your ears."

167

"Would you not tell? Don't tell Red."

He looked me over close like I was a test he knew he had to pass but he wasn't sure yet what the question meant. I'd hardly ever seen him worked up into a mad. He kept clicking his tongue while studying on me.

"I saw that shirt, I thought for a second you *were* Red."

"Got gas on mine."

"Yeah, well, somethin' here stinks of a sudden. Do you have an idea where he is? Do you? Answer me."

"How the fuck would I? He don't say boo to me most days. You know that's so, too."

"This ain't right." He stood there slouched, his hands and feet moving from one posture to another without settling on any. He shook his head in all the postures. "I just wonder since when do you got the *balls* to wear his stuff? Is it since you know he won't catch you? That's what makes sense to me. You know he ain't about to catch you."

"He won't if you don't tell. You don't *gotta* snitch, you know."

He spun about and trotted to the wall and jumped over it and into the Mustang and peeled off. I knew he'd go to the house. I turned the tractor around that way, too, but he'd be there long before me.

I pushed the old tractor as hard as I could. I pushed it hard over the old wrinkled ground. When I got close to the house I could see him yelling into the screen door. I could see his neck straining. I could not hear over the tractor noise. I figured she stood inside yelling back.

Once I came near enough and stopped the tractor all I heard was him: "That *proves* somethin' here stinks. You'd *never* tell me to stay away 'less you *knew* Red wasn't about to show and change your tune. Not in a million fuckin' years you wouldn't."

He gave me a tough look while getting into his car, then drove fast down the rutted lane. Me and her stared at each other, stared through the screen door instead of saying what needed to be said, then she turned away inside the house and I wheeled the tractor around to go any other way and went.

17

LATER ON I WAS LAYING in bed and found out I was moving. Found out all my tomorrows had been reshuffled. The sun still shined but was down to a glittering slit in the distance and I laid on top of the sheets, on my belly, watching the slit glitter and shrink. Him and her then came to the door, him behind, and stood there, him grinning, her not.

She said, "Name a place you always wanted to go."

"Me? Norway."

"Somewhere closer."

"Norway's for Vikings. That's for me."

"Name *closer* places."

"Okay. Chicago, Illinois."

"Name New Orleans. Try New Orleans."

"What's there?"

He said, "Tino's, bud. Tino's is a restaurant in what they call the French Quarter down there. It's a place where I'm just *liable* to be doin' the cookin' by next Monday."

"Remember *King Creole*, ho . . . Shug? That's New Orleans."

"It is?"

"Tino's is just practically on *Bour*-bon Street. That's the street everybody goes wild on. People from everywhere come there to get crazy. If you wanted to you could throw you an egg from Bourbon Street and probably come close to hittin' Tino's. It's just spittin' distance from The Dauphin."

"But why? Why go there?"

"You know we best not stay here. Don't act dumb."

"Fuck do I want with New Orleans?"

"I don't like that kind of talk in front of your mother. It's wrong for a boy to use words like that."

"I'm afraid he was taught to sound that way."

"What would we have, a boat, or what?"

"House. We'd have a house. They've got strange spooky houses. Olden foreign-style places with vines and big flowers."

"I'd get my own room?"

"Sure. Sure you would."

"And listen, boy, the food down there'll make you get swoony. You just walk down the street smellin' it and you'll get swoony. They're flat famous for their food, and they ain't famous for no good reason. The style of food down there is a wonderful challenge."

"Like what food?"

"Like shrimp big as chicken drumsticks."

"I've never even had any shrimps."

"Well, you'll be startin' at the top. This'll be the best shrimp you ever *will* have."

"Plus gumbo, Shug. French doughnuts. Pralines."

"And muffelettas."

"What the hell is one of them?"

"It's a sandwich they make. It's big as a pie. They put everything good they can think of on 'em. Oysters, olives, salami, shrimp, whatever. Take you an hour and a half to eat a whole one."

"I don't know about this. I don't know."

"Well, *I* know, Shug. I know this has to be. We have

got to go. We need to clear out and you *do* know it."

"When'll this be?"

"Soon as I get the call back from down there."

"Tino's gonna call?"

"Not Tino. Another fella I know. Tino's gone."

"I'd get all that food *and* my own room?"

"That's the plan."

"How 'bout a dog?"

"I don't know about dogs. Dogs are iffy. Their hair gets on my clothes. You know how I feel about that."

"*King Creole*," I said. "*King Creole*. Tell me about that sandwich again. It's called a *what*, now?"

18

THE WIND BLEW ROWDY and the white pillowcase flapped from my belt like one wing of a hurt bird flapping to raise me up the gutterpipe. A chisel sat in my ass pocket. That night there were beeves resting in the stockyard pens. I could see the pens from where I clung on the gutter. There'd been new wood laid to frame the doc's window. The wood was painted a quiet red color to chime with the bricks. The beeves hunkered in the pens very calm waiting for daylight when the butcher knives would find them. They did not stir or bawl. I stood on the ledge by the window and pulled the chisel. I studied the world from that height for a minute. The world looked the same as I always saw, only I could see more of it at a time. All those beeves just hunkered there waiting. That one wing flapped from my belt. I just raised a foot this time and stomped at the glass, then stomped the leftover jagged pieces from the new wood frame. The glass crashed and tinkled. The ol' doc was in a rough patch. The ol' doc was not raking it in I don't guess as he had tried to fix the old weak cabinets instead of buying the new strong kind. I went at them banging the chisel. They popped open with even fewer bangs than before. I filled the pillowcase until it showed a hefty lump, then tied it back onto my belt. I went to the gutterpipe and grabbed on and eased down. The white wing just hung on me then. No more flapping. The beeves would not stir even when I walked past them calling, "Moo!

Moo! This way, dumbasses, this way. Moo! Moo!" I went mooing clear around the town square past closed stores along dark sidewalks over to the street nearby where that Patty person lived. The white Mustang sat parked there at the curb. I opened the car door and emptied dope in bottles and bottles and boxes onto the passenger seat, then ran. It wasn't far to run but I let loose an awful stinky sweat from there to home.

19

GLENDA STOPPED CALLING ME HON. She also stopped throwing hugs to mark any good moment in a day. She took to only calling me Shug. Twice she tried to shift to Morris, Morris this, Morris this, too, but something about the sound of my legal name said out loud right away shifted her back to Shug, plain Shug.

Now and then she made promises about New Orleans: "You'll know people there you can't imagine now, Shug."

And: "Shug, there's a good chance you'll learn to sail a boat on the Gulf of Mexico."

And: "Why Shug, French doughnuts'll make you forget about most kinds of pie."

On this night the heat buckled at dark and she and me watched TV while a sprinkle of breeze pattered in through the screens. The show was supposed to be funny but the funny wasn't showing.

She said, "Where's the funny in that? What's funny about a four-eyed bum in a raincoat holdin' a flower? And that girl? That's not a real blond, even, and she can't tell a joke, or dance that great, either, but *she's* on TV."

The kitchen door squeaked open during the show and uneven footsteps brought Carl into the TV room. His clothes were all-white but sloppy, streaked by dirt, and the beer smell puffed about when he talked.

"Hey there," he said. He looked at the show a minute

but he laughed. He did not sit. For two seconds he tried to dance like the girl on the show. As he talked his words slowed and stretched into the shape dope makes words take. "Say, no sign of him yet?"

I said, "Not a shadow."

"Well now, ol' Ma's gettin' worried about her boy, you know."

"He'll show when he feels like it."

Glenda didn't say anything to him, and he stood there watching the show and laughing on his own. He saw jokes that slipped past her and me. During a commercial he grabbed my head hair and yanked so I had to look at him. He was most of the way boiled.

"Thought we'd go giggin'."

"You did?"

"Thought we'd gig a mess of frogs."

"Tonight?"

"This minute. Lace up your sneakers."

All Glenda said was, "Are you good to drive?"

"Yup. Yup."

"Okay—so go."

Carl drove Granny's station wagon. One headlight was winked shut and old newspapers and empty beer cans rolled and tinkled in the bed. I could not see any frog gigs but did see a rifle laid on the backseat. I poked the barrel hole with a finger and it felt to be a small-bullet rifle.

"Where'll we go to gig 'em?"

"This place."

As we reached the rock wall that edged the bone orchard he slammed the brakes, swatting up dust that swirled in the one headlight beam. The motor ticked.

He said, "Get in the middle."

Basil squirted from between the shadows there, opened the door and shoved me over.

"Scoot," he said. "Slide over, fatso."

Out along the road Basil said, "Got your *own* clothes on tonight." Just from his voice I knew his eyes were blurred by red streaks and his blood ran spiced with the ol' doc's dope. He made a point of slowly resting a pistol on the seat between his legs. I never before saw him to have a pistol. "Thought we'd powwow off in the woods, kid. Thought we'd powwow about stuff you might know and not be tellin'."

"I'm here to gig frogs."

"Could be you'll gig some. Could be. But first you'll answer up to us a little bit."

SHOT frogs were tossed in the wagon bed. Nobody brought gigs so the frogs were shot. The wagon sat parked with the headlight pointed skimming across the pond water to make frog eyes glow. The small bullets of the rifle planted small perfect holes with no splattering. The frogs weren't hard to see or hard to hit with the rifle. The pistol missed a lot more and threw squat burly bullets that ripped the frog bodies open and left shreds dangling. Their legs were all anybody wanted so which bullet hit their bodies made no big difference.

Carl and Basil wouldn't say much to me for a long while. Basil brought a little bottle holding a pale make of booze, and both of them were doped on pills. Even boiled Carl shot real good. Basil used the pistol like a drunk cowboy. When he saw frog eyes glow he strode towards the eyes blasting, making the water dance until a bullet chanced to catch a frog and ripped it open.

Carl said, "This is ol' Tribble's land. You know Tribble?"

Basil said, "The one with the eye?"

"The one with the house settin' on the far side of this ridge."

"He got both eyes?"

"This is a different Tribble from the one you think."

"I guess I don't, then."

The pond was a bowl in shape and shallow. Water lay in it the color of weak pea soup. Green stalks with thin leaves grew up around the rim of the pond. All I did was wade out between the green stalks and retrieve dead frogs until a nice mess of them had got shot and harvested. A long long stick helped me rake the frogs from the pond water to near the bank, where I fetched and tossed them in the wagon bed.

"When is it my shot?"

They both looked my way. They both held guns and looked my way with no helpful expressions showing from their faces. Neither stood too solid, but shuffled about like the world under their feet rippled and rolled.

Carl said, "I want you to know this. Over there I killed me two, or six, or maybe even eight motherfuckers who never did diddly to me. All they done was get their asses born where I was told to shoot. Read me? That's it. That's all. But still, I plumb *blew their shit up*! Shot their guts right out of 'em. So now, *Shug*, if it turns out to be somebody here at home greased my brother, then I want you to know I got somethin' special for the fuckers who done it."

"Wouldn't that make you a murderer?"

"So?"

"I'd hate to see you be a murderer."

"That ain't your choice to make."

Basil slipped over to me, pistol in his left hand so his right hand could grab me by the throat and choke. His eyes had that blur. His choke did not pack the oomph of Red's chokes.

"Tell me, fat boy. Who's the sport in the T-bird?"

He eased his grip on my throat.

"The *what* in the *what*?"

"Does your momma got her a new boyfriend that drives a Thunderbird?"

"*Thunder*-bird! I *wish*!"

He gave me a shaking by the throat, but it wasn't much of a shaking compared to others.

"Don't lie to me, kid. Don't do that."

I raised my hands and gave Basil a hard shove and stood back a step with my fists balled.

"You forgettin' who my daddy is?"

"You pushed me. See that? He pushed me. Tubby fuckin' punk."

I suppose I slid a step nearer to Carl.

"Don't try'n hog me down, Basil. Just 'cause you done a little time it don't mean you scare me."

Right then Carl laughed, which I know helped. His laugh helped let steam off. The laugh changed the tune. Basil sort of laughed, too.

"Dig the mouth on this punk, would you?"

"I heard him. I heard him. Sounds about like some-body else we know, don't he?"

After that they let me shoot the pistol twice. No frogs glowed for targets so I could only shoot the heart of the pond.

"Can't I shoot a few more?"

"Out of bullets," Basil said. "Next time, ol' son, we'll bring more."

The three of us had gone to sit in the wagon, and the engine ran, when shot frogs started hopping. Three or four frogs were shot but not dead. Their croaks wheezed. They hopped at the window glass and came down making wet slap sounds. The hops were duds, low and lame. The frogs landed strange, lurching like they had no balance left. We each sat watching silently as frogs we'd figured for good and dead kept trying to hop away.

"Je-sus," Carl said. "Grab 'em up. Bring 'em to me in the light."

Wounded frogs with no balance were simple to catch. I snatched them by their feet and carried them into the headlight beam. Carl held a hunting knife. Basil just sucked on his bottle and watched. Carl bent the legs over the blade and snapped the leg bones as the blade cut at the joint. He tossed the bodies into the pond. The bodies still made frog noises. The cutting and cracking only took a minute. The bodies croaked in the air and went thunk when they hit the pond water.

He said, "With no legs they'll drown."

20

WHAT SHE CAME TO SAY set loose my screams. The Thunderbird stopped near the screen door and she stepped out to come inside. The Thunderbird left and she came in carrying a sack from the ice cream store.

"You eat?"

"Supper—that dessert?"

"Banana split, Shug. Get it before it melts."

The table tilted this way and that while we sat. She smoked like always. I spooned and swallowed. The table tilted this way when I leaned over to spoon and that way when I sat up to swallow. I ate fast and the table tilted both ways.

"Call came from Tino's today. Jimmy Vin got the wrong answer."

"That's okay."

"Not really, it's not. We've got to get out of here, I feel sure of that. We can't stay, the way things are. He just now tried another call and this one answered right."

"So where to?"

"He'll be cookin' on a boat. The kind of boat that's as big as a grade school. So big you hardly feel the waves. Cookin' breakfast and tendin' bar at night. An ocean liner."

"When does this happen?"

"Once he gets his check tomorrow, it's, 'So long little ol' West Table, hello big ocean.'"

"That's awful fast. Ain't that awful fast?"

"The boat's got to leave on a certain schedule. It leaves out of Miami, then sails on to South America, that type of place. The boat goes down there and back, puttin' in at all the vacation islands spotted around in between."

"That sounds *good*. That sounds *great.*"

"I think it will be. I'm sure it will. You can't go."

"Huh?"

"You can't go. That's their rules."

"Don't. Don't."

"I *almost* couldn't go, but Jimmy Vin claimed we'd got married and I'd be useful in the galley, which is where he'll be. But there's no other room, Shug. You'll have to move in on Granny."

"Glenda? Glenda, you'll leave me easy as that? You'll just up and leave me alone?"

"No. No. Listen—you can move in on Granny."

I did not want to have feelings in front of anybody, nobody, which meant her.

"Is it because of in the kitchen? That time in the kitchen?"

"Don't work it around to where I'm mean. I'm not mean. Don't think that. But I need to start packin'— there's a lot to do."

"Is it because of in the kitchen? Is it?"

"You *toughen* up. Toughen up, and *hush.*"

"Everybody else does was why I done it."

"That's *not* why. You just can't go. *Hush.*"

THE bottle where I hid my lifelong screams busted

wide. The screams flew loose where nobody could hear. The road I walked along was sunburnt dirt and dust lifted with each step. I walked alone and felt my screams break free. I screamed over things that happened I thought I'd forgot. I screamed past fence rows and cows along the sunburnt road. Parts of me I did not understand broke loose inside and clogged my throat. The cows laid listening to my screams as if they knew all about them and didn't need to hear more. They looked towards me but did not stir. I climbed the fence going their way and let screams run among them. They laid near a creek bed dried white and cracked, a dry creek cut between banks of summer-white weeds. I screamed walking on the creek. It was a dry creek but the cracked bed had to lead somewhere. I sounded along the hard dry bed and around rocks and under trees that lisped and out again to bare pasture.

I screamed until my throat was whipped raw and the sun settled and set.

Then I walked home in the night, empty of feelings.

I climbed to the farthest dark corner of the tractor shed, in amongst the cobwebs and bat shit, and found the boot. I carried the boot under my arm like a loaf of bread and made my way along the town sidewalks past the town people doing all those things people did that do not matter. I went past them feeling raw and unknown.

At the shotgun shack where the Patty person lived I knocked hard on the door. Basil answered, shirt off, a can of beer in his hand.

"What, kid?"

There wasn't a bottle for my screams anymore.

I raised the boot and held it stretched between both hands so the eagle wings showed plain, and he began to cry.

21

ALL DAY I LET HER keep packing. She packed her things in cardboard boxes. I liked the way her hands moved folding clean clothes fresh from the line. I liked the way she hummed as her hands moved.

"Be sure and take those dresses he thinks you're so pretty in. Such a doll."

She packed six boxes of things she had to have.

She said to me once, "We'll be back this way in around a year. Maybe less."

I let her keep packing.

When she first noted he was late she said, "It's still early yet. He probably stayed for a goodbye drink with folks at the Echo. I'm sure that's where he is. It's not late yet."

She said to me once, "It won't be so bad at Granny's. You'll be off to the Marines in a few years."

The sun turned away like it was laughing at her. Sunset shoved her hope downhill. She kept her eyes on the lane through the bone orchard and watched and worried and sighed while nobody came.

I said, "Be sure'n comb your hair nice for him, now."

"The car must've broke down."

"That's gotta be it."

The more she was torn up the sweeter she got. I mixed her a thermos of tea. She kept her eyes on the lane as the night got darker.

"Johnny's on," I said. "Want to watch Johnny?"

I mixed her another thermos of tea when Johnny ended.

She said, "I don't know what the hell's goin' on. Maybe I don't want to know."

"You know what you need to know—he ain't comin'. He ain't comin' for you."

"You don't have to say it like that."

"You got dumped. Glenda, you got dumped. Jimmy Vin ain't goin' to show."

She was crushed. She was stomped flat. Her hope had gone under. She sat at the table with her head on her arms and let loose tears until they puddled beside her hands.

I pulled her raven hair back with my fingers to look her in the face as she wept.

"You ain't alone."

We went that way all night.

She said, "But you won't dump me, will you, hon?"

"Naw."

"You're different, hon. Aren't you? Aren't you different from the rest?"

"You raised me."

"But what'll we do for money?"

"I can get money."

"How is that, hon?"

"Never you mind how."

Through the night she got drunker and more attached to me. She hugged me plenty. We danced with no music until dawn was close. She rested her head on my shoulder. The smell of her was fine. Her lips brushed my neck.

I said, "I like the way you look best in that long-legged green thing you wear."

"Oh, baby, that thing is packed."

"I said I like *it* best."

I pushed through the screen door and out to the stoop. I sat to face the sun. She soon came to the screen and whispered to me. I turned to look at what she wore.

She'd heard me.

I raised my eyes to the sun and she came to stand behind me. I felt her knees in my back. There was something off about the sun. Not as round as normal but shining hard. All that sunshine coming my way and nothing I cared to see. I stared into the sun until I couldn't see a thing. I felt her fingers in my hair. I raised my hands, reached behind and stroked her long legs in the smooth smooth green thing. I stroked her legs all up and down. She did not move. I couldn't see a thing except a total blur of light. She did not move as my hands stroked higher.

I'd say no dawns ever did break right over her and me again.

Praise For Daniel Woodrell

"Daniel Woodrell is one of the major discoveries of the last decade."

—Time Out

"Echoes of William Faulkner and Erskine Cauldwell but Woodrell isn't imitating either of them. He's only drawing from the same well but with a different take, a different voice, a sharper sense of irony and satire."

—New York Times Book Review

"Daniel Woodrell can tell me a story any old time."

—Pinckney Benedict

"Woodrell is better than anyone at the vernacular of desperation, revenge and redemption, with dialogue as good as anything in Elmore Leonard and a skewed unpredictability reminiscent of Harry Crews."

—Uncut

Praise For Daniel Woodrell

"Woodrell is a marvellous writer."

—*Roddy Doyle*

"Daniel Woodrell is stone brilliant."

—*James Ellroy*

"This guy's an American original, like Cormac McCarthy. He has that old Testament sense of blood, vengeance and violence."

—*Philip Caputo*

"Woodrell alternates between reaming the language with a dry corncob and practising a particularly skilful kind of literary cabinetwork."

—*Annie Proulx*

"Woodrell throws down sentences that will leave you amazed."

—*Charles Frazier*

". . . some of the finest, toughest books in American fiction today."

—*John Williams*